THE WILD ONE

BY
LYN DENISON

Ferndale, Michigan
2000

Bella Books, Inc.
P.O. Box 201007
Ferndale, MI 48220

Printed in the United States of America on acid-free paper
First Edition

Editor: Lila Empson
Cover designer: Bonnie Liss (Phoenix Graphics)

ISBN 0-9677753-4-5

For Glenda, my LT

And for my long-suffering friends at Tuesday night OWLS who get to hear about the ups and downs of writing — even when they don't want to know

Chapter One

"I'm late! I'm late! I'm late!" Rachel Weston dropped her bag on the sofa and slid into the empty chair at the card table. "Sorry."

"Give her a fob watch and a pair of floppy ears and she'd be doing a credible White Rabbit." Rachel's cousin Colleen exclaimed.

Rachel joined in the laughter. "I really am sorry. I know I'm holding up the game."

"No worries, love," said her younger cousin, Sandy, as she shuffled the cards.

"So what upset your usually impeccable schedule?" asked Colleen.

"Impeccable schedule? What's that? You know I just keep on running and hope I don't blow a sneaker."

"Take no notice of Colleen, love. My sister just can't help being sarcastic. She was born that way. Fortunately it doesn't run in the family." Sandy continued shuffling the cards. "Anyway, what ran you late this time?"

Rachel rolled her eyes. "I had to drop into work on my way here."

"Work on your day off again?" exclaimed Rhonda, the fourth member of their fortnightly bridge club meeting. "Not pretty."

"Well, we're so behind." Rachel frowned. "If I don't get some staff soon we'll be in real trouble. I hate letting our customers down."

Colleen raised her eyebrows. "I thought you said you had a guy starting last week."

"I did. And although I had reservations about him, I thought he might be okay." Rachel grimaced. "I should have trusted my instincts. He only lasted two days."

They all looked taken aback, and Rachel shrugged. "Seems he didn't realize he'd have to get his hands dirty."

"Right," Colleen said in disbelief. "Working in a gardening and landscaping business? The guy must have been thick as two bricks."

"He said he thought he'd just be standing behind the counter and taking the money," Rachel explained wearily.

"How old was he?" Sandy asked.

"Thirty-something. Old enough to know better if he'd been at all serious about keeping the job." Rachel ran her hand through her short fair hair, momentarily surprised at its lack of length. She'd only had it cut two weeks ago and was still getting used to the new style after having had long hair since her teens. With the frantic pace of her life just recently, she'd decided a shorter style would be less trouble.

"Anyway," she continued, "he walked out when Phil asked him to help repot some seedlings. So I'm back to square one.

2

I don't know what I'd do without Phil and Ken and Old Dave."

"Can't you put on more part-timers?" suggested Rhonda. "I mean, you said Colleen's son and his friend were working in well."

"They are," Rachel conceded. "But they're both still at school and can only work on the weekends. That fits in really well Saturdays and Sundays, but no one seems to want to work part time during the week. What I really need is a couple of able-bodied men, one to work in the garden and supplies center with Phil and Old Dave, and one to help Ken with the landscaping. If I don't get someone soon we'll have to stop taking on new work. As it is we're over a month behind with the jobs we've got."

"You'd wonder it would be so difficult to get staff, what with the news always shouting about the rising number of unemployed," said Sandy. "But I guess not everyone wants to work outdoors with plants and stuff."

"And I suppose not everyone has a flair for it either," added Rhonda.

"Well, I for one would trade outdoors for trapped-in-a-room-with-thirty-twelve-year-olds any day, let me tell you," said Colleen with feeling. "Don't know how I did it full time for so many years. It wasn't until I reduced my hours that I realized how stressful it was."

"Does that mean I can put you on the payroll at R & R Gardening and Landscaping?" Rachel asked with a grin.

"Oh sure. And get my lily-white little hands all grimy and grubby." She winked at Rachel. "Now, Sandy's just about shuffled the numbers off the cards, so let's play this game."

The four friends settled into their game until they broke for lunch a couple of hours later.

"Quiche is ready," Rhonda called from the kitchen. "Go on out onto the deck. I've set the table for lunch out there."

Rachel, Colleen, and Sandy stood up and filed through the dining room and out onto the veranda. Rhonda followed them,

3

carrying the quiche. She set it on a warming board and proceeded to distribute healthy slices.

Each bridge day they rotated venues between their four houses, the hostess providing lunch.

"I'm so glad we take turns at being mother," Sandy said. "Otherwise I'd feel very guilty sitting back and letting you baby us like this, Rhonda."

"Oh yes?" Colleen sat down at the table on the deck. "You love every minute of it, just like we all do."

"Warming up a quiche hardly constitutes babying." Rhonda laughed easily. "Help yourselves to the salads."

"It's such a great day, warm but not too hot." Sandy added some crisp green salad to her plate. "Just the sort of day to eat out here on the deck. And the garden looks wonderful, Rhonda."

Rhonda grinned at Rachel. "Another one of Ken's successes. I'm glad I thought about getting him to clean the place up. Don't know why I didn't think of it sooner. He's a genius."

Rachel smiled. "He is pretty good at his job. I'm just terrified he'll want to leave and set up a business on his own."

"Maybe you should marry him and keep him in the family," Colleen suggested dryly. Rachel spluttered into her teacup.

"Marry him? Good grief, Col, I'm old enough to be his mother."

"Rubbish! He must be pushing thirty and you're only, what? Thirty-something?"

"Thirty-three. Eleven months younger than you are," Rachel added with relish.

"That's the trouble with small towns, isn't it?" laughed Sandy. "Everyone knows everything about you."

"That's true. There aren't many secrets here." Rhonda passed Colleen sugar for her coffee. "But, Sandy, I thought you were all fired up matchmaking Rachel with your brother-in-law, Phil. I seem to recall you saying Rachel and Phil were made for each other."

"Sandy's been trying to manage that ever since Phil came back to town." Colleen pulled a face at her cousin. "To no avail. Rachel will resist."

"Phil works for me and does a great job. I just don't think it's sensible to mix business with pleasure."

"Well, that's a step in the right direction, isn't it, Sandy?" Colleen appealed to her sister. "At least she now admits it's pleasure."

Rhonda patted Rachel's knee. "Leave poor Rachel alone. It is only four years since Rob died, and she needs to work through that. Rachel will know when she's ready to commit herself to another relationship."

Rachel took another mouthful of Rhonda's delicious quiche and wondered if it was quite that simple. When Rob, her husband of seven years, was killed in a motor accident, it seemed to Rachel that her whole existence had taken on a numbness, a sort of unreality.

Not that she'd had time to dwell on it. With two young children and a fledgling business to run, life had spun on with unrelenting ruthlessness. It had been a case of putting one foot in front of the other and carrying on.

Rachel grimaced inwardly. Thinking that way made her feel like a modern day martyr. But that wasn't the case. She'd simply not had time to think too much, and now she seemed incapable of thinking too far ahead.

What worried her the most was that recently she'd begun to feel as though her marriage was just a figment of her imagination. She was often hard-pressed to remember Rob, how she felt about him, about their marriage.

Oh, she knew they hadn't had a bad marriage. It hadn't set her pulses racing the way pulses raced in romantic novels, but she knew Rob had basically been a good man. And she had loved him. She knew she had. Otherwise she wouldn't have married him. Would she?

"Oh, I almost forgot." Sandy's voice drew Rachel out of her disquieting reflections. "Guess who Steve saw in town the other day?"

"Your husband never sees anyone in town, Sandy," said Colleen. "Just last week he walked straight past me and didn't even blink an eyelid. Talk about an absent-minded accountant."

"I know." Sandy sighed in agreement. "Sometimes he's the bane of my life. He spends all week in town at his office, and he never, but never, hears any juicy gossip. Well, maybe he hears it, but he sure doesn't pass it on to me. If it wasn't for our bridge game I'd be entirely gossipless."

"Now that doesn't bear thinking about, does it?" Rachel put in wryly.

"Don't you talk, Rachel," stated Colleen. "You're almost as closemouthed as Steve. Now stop distracting Sandy." She turned to her sister. "So who *did* Steve see in town the other day that made such an impression on him he broke his silence to tell you all? I mean, I can't even contemplate the scenario where Steve stands chatting in the street and then hurries home to tell you about it, Sandy."

"Well, there were extenuating circumstances. Steve did go to school with him."

"That narrows it down." Rhonda laughed. "So, who do we know who's male, stayed in town after high school, and is Steve's age?"

"We'd be flat-out naming two or three," said Colleen. "So tell us more."

"Well, actually, he's older than Steve."

"Sandy! Keep to the point!" instructed her sister shortly in her schoolteacher tone.

"Johnno Farrelly," Sandy said without preamble.

"And?" Colleen prompted. "I often see Johnno around. The

6

Farrelly brothers have done really well for themselves since they took over their father's business. They've made a real go of it. Now there's a success story."

"Johnno runs the office, but Liam still drives the trucks though, doesn't he?" asked Rhonda.

Sandy nodded. "Strange, isn't it? Both Johnno and Liam Farrelly are married and have made good lives for themselves. With their family life you wouldn't be surprised if they'd turned out bad through and through."

"Bad genes *do* seem to run in families." Colleen put in.

"Well Becky, the older sister, she's still working at the hospital," added Rhonda. "I often see her. She's a good worker, married with three kids. She's a really nice woman."

"I suppose three out of four good ones in that original screwed-up family isn't bad," said Colleen caustically.

Rachel took another sip of her tea, suddenly just a little ill at ease. Yet she couldn't say why. She felt dissociated, as though the conversation was going on around her and she wasn't exactly a part of it.

Of course Rachel knew the story of the Farrellys. Everyone did. The family had been the brunt of local gossip for as long as Rachel could remember. Rachel knew it was common knowledge that Old Will Farrelly, Johnno's grandfather, had been a drinker and quick with his fists. Often his exploits had been rationalized because he was supposed to have had a bad time during the war, some sort of war neurosis, Rachel had once heard her mother telling someone. But Rachel wondered why that had been an acceptable excuse for beating his wife and children.

Old Will's daughters had all left town as soon as they were old enough, but young Will, the only son, stayed and drove trucks for his father. He drank like his father, fought like he did. And when Will Jr. had started courting a very young Laura Driscoll, no one could believe she would actually go out with him. He was six years older than she was and had a wild reputation.

But they had married, and young Will had continued to provide plenty of food for local gossip until his death years ago.

"You mean she's back?"

There was a moment of shocked silence, and Rachel blinked. She'd obviously missed something while she was woolgathering.

"Who?" she asked evenly, valiantly trying to ignore an inexplicable, growing hollowness as a disturbing seed of premonition began to take form somewhere inside her. "Who's back?"

Colleen raised her eyebrows. "Who's back? Pay attention, Rachel. Quinn Farrelly. That's who."

"She" — Rachel swallowed — "she is?"

"That's what Johnno told Steve," Sandy explained.

"Wow!" Rhonda exclaimed. "Has she just been released from prison, do you suppose?"

Sandy frowned. "I shouldn't think so. It all happened, what, ten, twelve years ago? She only got three years, didn't she?"

"Yes. I think it was three years," Rachel said carefully. "So she should have been released years ago."

"You'd think if she was going to come back here she would have done so when her mother died a couple of years ago." Rhonda started clearing away their lunch dishes.

"Broke her mother's heart, that one," said Colleen softly.

"She was young," Rachel put in before she could stop herself. Her cousin turned to look at her.

"You always did stand up for her, Rach, and I could never understand why."

Rachel shrugged. "I just think she had a raw deal. It can't have been easy growing up in that household, with a father like Will Farrelly."

Sandy nodded. "I'd have hated it, having everyone know what a drunken no-good my father was, that he beat my

8

mother. Heaven only knows what those kids went through. No wonder Quinn had problems."

"Problems?" Colleen shook her head. "She was a tearaway from the moment she started to walk. I taught her one year and, let me tell you, that was no picnic."

"I just think she was smart enough to do anything with her life," Rachel said. "It was such a pity it all turned out the way it did. Such a waste."

"Oh, Quinn was smart enough. Maybe too smart." Colleen stood up and began to help Rhonda clear the table. "As I see it, she just inherited those bad family genes. Quinn Farrelly was just like her father and grandfather before her. She was a wild one."

Chapter Two

Rachel had planned to go into the office for an hour or so after her bridge game but she decided to head on home. For some reason she felt absolutely exhausted.

She pushed the button on her mobile for Phil's home number and waited for him to pick up.

"Phil here." Phillip Stevens's deep voice echoed metallically inside the car.

"Oh. Hi, Phil. It's Rachel. I just wanted to ask you if Kirby rang to say the seedlings arrived okay."

"Yeah. Rang just after lunch. Another satisfied customer."

"That's a relief. I'm glad he's happy with them."

"Why wouldn't he be happy?" Phil asked. "They got quality merchandise and a good deal."

"So did we, my friend." Rachel sighed. "Well, I'll see you in the morning."

"Rachel? Hang on a minute."

"Something else?"

"Yeah. Someone called in about a job."

Rachel pulled up at a stop sign. "They did? Who?" The phone crackled with static.

". . . came in just after you left . . . was with a customer so I didn't . . . Old Dave made it nine-thirty in the morning. That okay with you?"

"You're breaking up. Was that nine-thirty for an interview?"

"Yeah. CV's in the top drawer of your desk. Okay?"

"That's fine, Phil. I'll look at it when I get to work. Thanks again."

"No worries. Bye."

Rachel switched off the mobile. She wasn't going to let herself get excited about the job applicant. After the last fiasco she was beginning to doubt her judgment of people.

These were the times she missed Rob. He was so laid back about that sort of thing. Rob would have taken it all in his stride. She missed that.

She felt a twinge of guilt. Was that the only time she missed her late husband? When she felt she needed support doing something she didn't care to do, like taking the kids to the dentist and interviewing new staff?

Well, not exactly, she told herself. In truth she knew they'd occasionally had disagreements because Rachel thought Rob was too unconcerned about everything. Rob never seemed to worry about their overdraft, when they had one in the early days, or the mortgage payments or new shoes for the kids.

Rachel knew she'd worried enough for both of them — and felt ill-used about it. It had taken her a long time to reign in her tendency to be overanxious. She supposed the money she'd inherited when her father died had helped in that respect.

11

It hadn't been a fortune, but it had paid off their house mortgage and most of their bills. And apart from the loan for their business, the money had put them in the black for the first time since their marriage.

They'd also renovated the house slightly so that Rob's widowed mother could have her own self-contained flat attached to their house. Rob's mother had helped look after the children when Rachel was at work at the garden center. It had worked so well.

By the time Rob's mother remarried a year before Rob's death, the children had been old enough to spend the few hours after school with a qualified childcare giver.

Rachel turned the station wagon into her driveway and paused to look at the house. She'd fallen in love with it when she and Rob first saw it just before they were married.

It was a two-story brick home on a large block in a new estate. Of course, after ten years the estate had become a complete little settlement of middle to upmarket homes. The gardens Rachel had lovingly planned and planted were well established. Just before Rob's death they'd added a swimming pool in the back.

The house was too big for them really, Rachel reflected as she waited for the double garage door to glide open. But she still loved the place, felt a pleasant relief of tension as she arrived home.

She parked the car, and the door slid down behind her. The other car bay was empty, even more so at the moment with the children's bicycles gone. Fliss and Adam were spending some time on the farm with their grandmother and step-grandfather. The children loved visiting the farm and spent as much of their school vacations there as Rachel would allow.

Rachel checked her mail while she waited for the kettle to boil. Then she carried her tea into the living room and sank into her favorite chair. Kicking off her shoes, she stretched her bare feet out on the coffee table. She grimaced. Not the most elegant of poses, but who was there to see her?

The house sighed quietly, and Rachel tossed the mail aside. Nothing interesting.

She sipped her tea in the silence. Maybe she should do something about letting the flat again.

She glanced at the door off the living room. It led to the self-contained flat consisting of a large bedroom with an *en suite*, a kitchenette, and a living room.

The last tenants, two young students from the Agricultural College, had rented it during the school year, but they'd finished their courses weeks ago and had left for home or jobs elsewhere. In a few weeks there would be another influx of students, so Rachel knew she'd have no trouble finding a tenant or tenants.

Her mother had said she was taking a chance letting strangers rent the flat, but so far Rachel had had no trouble. And having the flat occupied had made the house feel more, well, filled. Since Rob died the house had taken on a slight emptiness. Physically, Rob had been a tall, broad-shouldered man, and he seemed to fill the house with his presence.

It was a strange feeling. But during the years they were married, Rachel had often felt Rob overwhelmed her, smothered her somehow. Wherever he was, Rob was usually surrounded by noise. Now Rachel realized guiltily that she enjoyed the silence.

But just knowing someone was in the flat made the house feel lived in. Maybe she appreciated the silence but missed the actual presence. Sort of the best of both worlds, she supposed.

She stood up and returned to the kitchen and made herself prepare a light snack. After her big lunch with her bridge club she didn't feel like another heavy meal. She settled on a light salad and carried her plate through to the dining room.

She was halfway through her meal when she suddenly found herself thinking about Quinn Farrelly. She set her fork down and rested her chin on her hand.

If she were totally honest with herself she'd have to admit that Quinn Farrelly had been flitting about on the periphery of her thoughts ever since Sandy had mentioned Quinn's return.

Rachel could picture Quinn as clearly as though she had seen her yesterday rather than almost a dozen years ago. *And why wouldn't she remember her?* she asked herself. She'd known Quinn all her life. Well, just about all her life. From the time Rachel and her mother had moved back to her mother's hometown when Rachel's parents had divorced. Rachel had been eleven years old then, so that constituted most of her life.

They'd attended the same local primary school, although Quinn was three years behind Rachel. Then they'd gone on to different high schools, Quinn to the state high school and Rachel to a private girls' school in Ipswich. They'd crossed paths occasionally in the township or at interschool sports meets.

Quinn was one of her school's sports stars, while Rachel was lousy at sports. Yet Rachel had always watched any games Quinn had played. Netball. Softball. Hockey. Swimming. Quinn was a member of all the teams over the years. Rachel often wondered when Quinn found time to attend all the practice sessions on top of keeping up with her schoolwork, because Quinn did reasonably well in the classroom too. What did they call it? An all-rounder. Quinn Farrelly was a good all-rounder.

They lost touch while Rachel was away at university, but when Rachel was sent to the local state high school as a student teacher, the first face to swim out of the sea of students in her first class was that of Quinn Farrelly. Quinn, with her hennaed hair standing up in a spiky cut, full lips smiling crookedly, gray eyes levelly meeting Rachel's.

Rachel had been excruciatingly nervous and, of course, the class of sixteen- and seventeen-year-olds had immediately tuned into her fear. Rachel knew they were going to give her a hard time and she very nearly panicked and ran for her life. But she managed to hold on to her composure long enough to introduce herself, and it had been Quinn who, Rachel suspected, had saved her.

She'd stood up and welcomed Rachel, reminded her peers that Rachel had gone to school with their siblings, made it sound as though Rachel was "one of them." Things seemed to have gone on relatively smoothly after that. Thanks to Quinn Farrelly.

Later in the staff room one of Rachel's fellow teachers had sympathetically asked Rachel how she'd managed the class. When Rachel had gratefully sung Quinn's praises, there had been a moment of telling silence before various exclamations of disbelief.

"Quinn Farrelly?" exclaimed one teacher. "Don't trust that little minx. She's just lulling you into a false sense of security."

"She's a troublemaker, that one," agreed another.

Only May Stokes, the oldest woman on the staff, had made anything like a positive comment on Quinn. "Quinn's not so bad, considering," she'd said, looking over her half-glasses. Everyone else had laughed skeptically. Only later, after what happened, had May Stokes elaborated on her statement as she'd sat beside Rachel at the trial.

Who could blame the child? May Stokes had expressed her compassion for Quinn to Rachel. A nonexistent home life. A drunken, abusive father who had been in and out of jail. A family who didn't seem to care what sort of friends Quinn made, where or how she spent her time. Was it any wonder Quinn Farrelly had earned her dreadful nickname? The Wild One.

Chapter Three

Rachel locked the station wagon and hurried into the office. As usual, Phil had the coffee brewing. Rachel sighed appreciatively.

"That smells divine," she said as Phil handed her a steaming mug.

"Saw you pull into the car park and knew you would have skipped breakfast again."

"What makes you think that?" Rachel asked after her first sip of coffee. "And what do you mean, 'skipped breakfast again'?"

"I could hear your tummy rumbling from here."

Rachel put her hand on her stomach. "You could not. My tummy never rumbles."

"Whatever you say, boss." Phil shrugged and offered her a plate of warm muffins. "Apart from that, the kids are at their grandparents', so I knew you wouldn't take the time for breakfast."

Rachel looked at the muffins. They were blueberry, her favorite, and she only hesitated a second before she took one, murmuring her appreciation as she bit into its softness.

"I know I've said it before, but you make the best muffins in the world, Phil. Although heaven only knows when you find the time."

"It's all in the organization and planning," he said and munched on his own muffin. "And talking about organization and planning, you'd be better served taking time for breakfast and calling in to see Ken during work hours. Or better still, just phone him. You know I can handle opening the shop here, so there's no point in rushing about. Breakfast is the most important meal of the day."

"This is the first time I've missed breakfast all week," Rachel got in before he could continue. "And it was only because I'd overslept."

And she'd overslept because she'd tossed and turned for hours before she'd finally dozed off. She'd found it so difficult to relax. Her thoughts had kept returning to Quinn Farrelly.

Every time Rachel had closed her eyes she'd seen Quinn's face. Her long, lithe body. Her clear gray eyes. And her mouth, with its quirky smile that was so naively young and yet so cynically adult at one and the same time.

Just remembering her nighttime recollections started an unsettling warmth growing in the pit of Rachel's stomach. She pulled her thoughts back to the present.

"And how did you know I'd called in to see Ken anyway?" she asked Phil.

He touched his finger to the side of his nose and then grinned. "Because Ken rang to say he forgot to tell you he'd be needing the Bobcat at the Graingers' tomorrow."

"I've got that all organized." Rachel licked the last muffin crumbs from her fingers. "I rang Bill Parsons yesterday, and he said he'd be at the job site at eight-thirty A.M. He's got a small job first thing, and then he'll go straight over to our job." Rachel took another sip of her coffee and then set the mug down on her desk. "I'll ring Ken and tell him."

"I'll do that. You finish your coffee before the first customers start storming the battlements."

A rusty utility drove into the car park, and Phil pulled a face. "Oops! Too Late! You gulp down your coffee and I'll phone Ken. Another day, another dollar."

Rachel laughed and went out to greet one of their regulars.

An hour later Rachel was still attending to what had turned out to be an influx of customers. The last one, old Mrs. Jorgenson, had bought some new ground cover for her prize-winning garden.

"Let me carry these out to your car for you," Rachel said, picking up the cardboard box of rose mulch and plants and following the old lady out to the car park.

"This is kind of you, Rachel." Mrs. Jorgenson beamed as she opened the boot of her ancient Ford.

Rachel set the box carefully on the original carpet. Then she closed the lid. "They'll be flowering before we know it, once your green thumb gets to work."

"Green thumb or not, there's only one reason I shop here, Rachel. I know I'm your mother's friend, but I come because you have good quality plants, love. Makes all the difference. And your special rose mulch is one of my garden's best-kept secrets. Of course, I get friendly service, too," she added with a smile.

Rachel mimed a salute. "We aim to please, ma'am."

"Should be more like you, Rachel," Mrs. Jorgenson said as she settled behind the wheel. "Most people these days don't understand the meaning of service any more." She waved and drove away.

The car park was empty for the first time since they

opened. Rachel sighed with relief as she headed back inside the gate. Maybe now she could finish her cold coffee.

At that moment a loud, throaty roar made her pause and look around. A battered yellow Gemini that had seen better days turned into the gateway.

"Famous last words," Rachel muttered to herself. The car had obviously blown a muffler and surely wouldn't pass a police mechanical inspection.

Rachel walked into the office and glanced out the window but only caught sight of a jean-clad leg as the Gemini's driver headed in through the gates. Rachel looked at her watch. Nine-twenty-five. It seemed like only a moment ago she'd arrived at work. Where had the hour and a half gone?

Nine-twenty-five? Oh no. She'd forgotten the job interview Phil had set up. And so had Phil, otherwise he would have reminded her. The applicant would be here any minute, and she hadn't so much as glanced at the résumé he'd left her.

She sat down, opened her drawer, and only had time to set the CV on her desktop before there was a knock on the doorframe. Phil stuck his head into the office.

"Lucky things have slowed down." He grimaced apologetically. "Your job applicant is here."

"Already?" Rachel gave a soft groan. "I haven't . . ." She sighed resignedly. "Okay. Better send him in."

"It's a her, actually," said a husky voice. A tall woman stepped around Phil and into the office.

Chapter Four

The woman wore dark boots, dress jeans with knife-edged creases, a white shirt with the collar unbuttoned at the throat, and a light, blue-toned checked jacket. And she seemed to have the longest legs Rachel had ever seen.

Her dark hair was short, layered back over the sides of her head, the top spiking, a few strands falling onto her forehead. And Rachel would have known her anywhere. Her face seemed thinner, had lost the roundness of adolescence, but the clear gray eyes were the same.

Yet now that Rachel was over the initial shock of seeing her again, she realized the intervening twelve years had added more than mere maturity. Her eyes might be the same arresting shade of gray, but some of the burning brightness

Rachel remembered had gone from them, her tentative smile only touching her full lips.

Quinn Farrelly. Quinn Farrelly was here. Wanting a job.

And all at once Rachel wanted to tidy her hair. Her hand moved upward, and she disguised the movement by nervously adjusting the collar of her shirt.

"Quinn. Hello. I, you're . . ." Rachel cringed inwardly and valiantly drew herself together. "You're home," she finished banally.

"You two know each other?" Phil asked, looking questioningly from one to the other.

"Sort of." Quinn gave a soft laugh that played over Rachel's skin, making the fine hair on her arms prickle.

Rachel swallowed as her throat threatened to close. What was wrong with her? She'd known Quinn was home. Why was it such a surprise she'd be looking for a job?

"We went to school together," Quinn was telling Phil.

"You did?" Phil looked surprised.

"Only just." Rachel's vocal cords were tight, too, and she swallowed again. "I was a few years ahead of Quinn."

"What a coincidence." Phil held out his hand. "I'm Phil Stevens. I work here, and I'm sort of Rachel's cousin-in-law."

Quinn raised her eyebrows.

"My brother's married to Rachel's cousin," Phil added, and Quinn nodded.

"Ah. The teacher or Sandy?"

"Sandy."

"Stevens?" She frowned slightly. "You must be the older brother who was in the Navy, and this brother of yours would have to be Steve then. Right?"

Phil laughed. "Yes, I was in the Navy and, yes, Steve's my brother. My younger brother. Can you believe our parents named him Steven Stevens? I've always been relieved they didn't think of it when I was born."

Quinn laughed again. "I remember him. He's a nice guy."

"All the Stevenses are like that," Phil said jauntily.

"All?" Quinn teased. "How many are there?"

"Just Steve and me."

They laughed easily together, and Rachel moved slightly, her chair creaking on its wheels. Both Quinn and Phil turned to look at her, the smile fading just slightly on Quinn's face.

"So. You're here to apply for a job?" Rachel asked in what she hoped was a businesslike tone.

Quinn inclined her head. "I left my résumé here yesterday. With Old Dave Smith."

Phil rubbed his hands together. "How about some coffee? Rachel? Quinn?"

They both declined.

"Okay. I'll leave you two to it then." Phil raised his eyebrows hopefully at Rachel before he left.

Now that Phil was gone, Rachel perversely wanted to call him back. She felt decidedly hot. And unprepared. How she wished she'd looked at Quinn's CV earlier. At least then she'd have been forewarned.

"Please. Won't you sit down." She indicated the other chair, and Quinn stepped forward, and sat in the chair on the other side of Rachel's desk.

She casually crossed one booted foot over the other and relaxed back into the chair.

Rachel wished she had the other woman's composure. She was a mass of nerves, and her stomach churned as much as it would if she'd been the interviewee rather than the interviewer. She'd always been inclined to be that way. Even more so since she'd had to handle the business on her own.

Yet it was more than that.

And if Rachel's thoughts the evening before had disturbed her sleep, then she suspected seeing Quinn again would be responsible for ongoing insomnia. Seeing Quinn brought back even more memories, memories Rachel thought she'd safely buried, never to be allowed to resurface.

Quinn Farrelly was still as attractive, as striking, as she'd always been. Impossibly more so. But Rachel quickly pushed that thought to the very back of her mind. She'd think about that later.

To cover her uneasiness she opened the résumé that lay on the desk in front of her. She scanned the printed document, but she had trouble concentrating on the words. All she could see was Quinn's name. Quinn Maryann Farrelly.

"I haven't, I mean . . ." Rachel swallowed and closed the résumé. "Why don't you tell me . . ." Rachel's throat closed again.

"Why I want the job?" Quinn finished easily.

Rachel made herself smile, forcing herself to act as normally as Quinn was. "Well, for a start."

"Okay. Last week my sister, Becky, was talking to someone who had been talking to your cousin, Sandy, and she told Becky that Sandy said you needed staff pretty desperately. I also need work desperately." Quinn pulled a rueful face. "It sounded like some sort of good omen. You needing staff, me needing a job. And I prefer to work outdoors, so this job sounded ideal." She stopped and gave a quick laugh. "What I should be saying is that I've had experience in this line of work."

Rachel glanced at the résumé and back at Quinn.

Quinn sighed softly. "As you know, I've been in prison. For five years, three months, one week, and two days, to be exact." She grimaced again and gave a self-derogatory smile. "I was counting, believe me."

She sat up a little straighter. "For the last part of my sentence I was at the prison farm. I guess you could say that saved my sanity, and I learned a lot. Then for several years after my release I had a job in a plant nursery in northern New South Wales, and when I came back to Queensland I also worked in a well-established hydroponic vegetable market garden. That was last year." She indicated the résumé. "I have references."

Rachel tried to get herself into business mode. "And why did you leave that position?"

23

Quinn's expression barely changed. "There was a change of ownership and a reshuffling of staff. A few of us, those who were hired last, were let go. The previous owners gave me a good reference though. It's in my résumé. Apart from that, I'd been wanting to come home for some time, so it seemed like a good opportunity."

Rachel opened the CV again and scanned Quinn's employment history. Apart from one-five month period, Quinn had been working the entire time since she had left prison. Rachel wondered why Quinn hadn't come home when she got out of jail. According to her résumé, that would have been about seven years ago. Surely . . .

"You didn't come home after your release?" she heard herself asking.

Quinn looked down, brushed at an imaginary speck of dust on the leg of her jeans. "No," she said, and her gaze met Rachel's again. "No. At the time I didn't think that was an option."

The telephone rang, and Rachel jumped. "Excuse me," she said as she fumbled with the receiver.

"Rachel?" her mother-in-law said before Rachel could identify herself.

"Rose. What's wrong?" Rachel's fingers tightened on the receiver. Had something happened to the children?

"Nothing's wrong, my dear. Stop being such a worrywart," said Rose Danielson. "I'm just ringing to tell you that you don't have to drive up to collect the children on Friday night. Charlie and I are coming down to see the new grandson, so we'll drop them off and save you the trip."

"Vicki's had her baby?" Rachel asked with a smile, and Rose chuckled.

"Just this morning. A boy. Eight pounds. Both well. And everyone's ecstatic."

"I can imagine. Of course, I don't know how the little guy is going to cope with having four big sisters," Rachel added.

"That's what Charlie said. But he's just thrilled to bits.

It's only his second grandson. Although you know he adores the girls."

"I know. All what? Eighteen of them, isn't it?" Rachel laughed. "That must be some sort of record."

"Probably. Anyway, we're coming down to see them on Friday, and we thought it would be easier for you if we dropped Fliss and Adam in to the garden center after we've been to the hospital. The children want to see the baby too. Is that all right with you?"

"That's fine, Rose. Thanks. Oh, and give my congratulations and best wishes to Vicki and Tim when you see them."

"I will. Good-bye, my dear."

Rachel put down the receiver and smiled at Quinn. "That was my mother-in-law. A couple of years ago Rose married Charlie Danielson, from Daydawn Farm. They were both widowed, and" — Rachel shrugged — "anyway, Charlie's son and his wife have just presented him with his twentieth grandchild."

"Twentieth! It must be bedlam when the whole family visits."

"It is." Rachel laughed. "Add mine to Charlie's twenty, and you can forget a football team. We're heading for an entire football game."

"You have children?"

"Yes. Two, would you believe? Felicity's ten and Adam's eight."

"I've got a daughter myself," Quinn said, and Rachel was more than a little surprised.

"You have?"

"Katie." Quinn's expression softened. "She's just five. Starts school in the New Year." Quinn's smile widened. "Katie's, well, she's a great kid."

Rachel smiled too, wondering if the child's father had come back with Quinn. The idea filled her with a mass of conflicting emotions.

They were both silent for a moment.

"Did your, did Katie's father . . . What does your husband think of your hometown?" Rachel was horrified to hear herself ask.

Quinn looked down at her hands. "Katie's father and I aren't together any more."

"Oh. I'm sorry."

Quinn nodded. "It didn't work out." Her fingers worried at the crease in her jeans. "So you married Rob Weston?"

Rachel sobered. "Yes. Nearly eleven years ago."

"I didn't think you liked him when he pursued you in high school."

"You remember that?" Rachel shrugged. "I guess he improved with time," she said as lightly as she could.

"And his persistence paid off."

Rachel grimaced. "I don't know about that."

"He was always keen on you, although, as I said, I didn't think his ardor was reciprocated."

Rachel shrugged. "We had a good marriage," she said carefully. Quinn glanced away again.

"Becky told me he was killed a couple of years ago."

"Yes."

"That must have been hard for you."

Rachel nodded. For some reason she didn't want to discuss Rob with Quinn. It made her feel almost guilty somehow. She pulled herself together and picked up Quinn's résumé again. "So. Where were we?"

"I was just about to beg you for this job," Quinn said lightly, and her low teasing tone unsettled Rachel again.

"Oh no. Please don't. I hate to see a woman beg." Rachel tried to match Quinn's lightness.

Quinn laughed and stood up. "Me too. Especially when it's me." She walked over and looked out the door at the garden center. "You have a great setup here. Old Dave showed me around the plant nursery here yesterday, and he told me you have gardening supplies next door and also a landscaping company as well."

"Yes, we do. Ken Leeson runs that part of the business, and we're short of staff there too, so part of the job may include having to help out with Ken as well. It's very physical, I'm afraid."

"I'm pretty wiry, and I'm willing to learn."

Rachel couldn't prevent herself from letting her gaze move quickly over Quinn's tall body. She did look strong and fit. And . . . Rachel swallowed quickly. "Yes, well, most of your work would be here. We're looking for someone to work with Ken full time, but we haven't found anyone suitable yet. Unless you know someone else who wants work?" she asked half jokingly.

Quinn frowned slightly. "Actually I do. My nephew, Kerrod. Johnno's eldest. He's just turned seventeen and finished high school this year."

"He's not interested in the family business?" Rachel asked.

"No. And Johnno's pretty good about it. I think he's pinning his family business hopes on his second son, to go into the trucking business. I could see if my nephew's interested if you like."

"Okay. Ask him to give me a ring." Rachel looked down over Quinn's résumé. Her references were glowing. No prospective employer could doubt that. But Quinn Farrelly had spent time in prison.

"The contact numbers in there are all current, and any of my references would be pleased to talk to you about my work. Or if you just want to check any of it," Quinn said.

Rachel nodded, flushing slightly, feeling as though Quinn

had read her mind. There was no reason why Rachel should be hesitating in giving Quinn the job. She was more than qualified. But . . .

"I hope my jail time isn't a problem," Quinn said then, and Rachel looked up at her.

"No. No, of course not." She turned another page, knowing her flush was deepening. Rachel knew her reservations had nothing to do with Quinn's prison record. They went far deeper than that, were far more confidential.

And if Quinn knew that Rachel's reticence had nothing to do with her prison record . . . Yet, in fairness, Rachel knew she couldn't jeopardize Quinn's job chance because of her own personal confusion all those years ago.

Rachel made herself concentrate on the words on Quinn's résumé. "You have a Bobcat license?" she asked in surprise.

"Bobcat. Forklift. Loader." Quinn shrugged. "I'm a woman of many talents."

"You can operate the loader over in the supplies yard?"

"I'm sure I could."

"And coming from a trucking background, I don't suppose our delivery truck would be a problem?"

Quinn grinned. "None at all."

"Now this *is* impressive." Rachel smiled. "I guess that settles it. When can you start?"

Quinn's grin widened, and she crossed back to stand in front of Rachel's desk. "How about tomorrow?"

"Fine." Rachel stood up, and when Quinn held out her hand Rachel automatically reached across the desk.

Quinn's handshake was firm, and Rachel was very aware of the warmth of her fingers, a warmth that lingered after Quinn had released her.

Chapter Five

"There are stacks of forms to fill out," Rachel said quickly, turning away to open a filing cabinet behind her desk. Her heart was thundering away inside her chest, and she took extra time collecting the papers to regain her composure.

"What would we do without all the bureaucratic red tape?" Quinn said as Rachel handed her the forms.

"Have a much less stressful life. I would, anyway. The paperwork around here is the bane of my life. Want to fill the forms out now?"

Quinn shrugged. "Sure. Why not?"

"Oops! Nearly forgot." Rachel handed Quinn another form and explained about ordering her uniform. They all wore dark green shorts in summer with a light green tailored shirt, and slacks and a jacket in winter.

"We provide the uniforms, so there's no expense to you involved and our supplier will have the shirts personalized with your name in a couple of days." She pointed to the breast pocket of her own shirt where her name was embroidered in dark green above R & R Landscaping. Quinn's gaze settled on Rachel's breast and, although Rachel knew Quinn's interest was innocent reflex action, Rachel felt the tingle of awareness in the pit of her stomach. Hastily she pulled herself together.

"Why not sit around here at my desk?" she added quickly. "It will be easier to do the paperwork. When you're finished, come outside and I'll give you a more extensive tour than Old Dave did yesterday."

"Sure." Quinn smiled again, and Rachel turned and hurried out of the office and into the garden center, her mind a whirling mass of chaotic confusion.

"Sorry I forgot to remind you about the interview." Phil materialized beside Rachel and she shrugged. "So?" he prompted eagerly. "What do you think? Will she do?"

"I think so," Rachel replied carefully. Phil was more than a little enthusiastic. She glanced sideways at him. He was an attractive man, as Rachel's cousin, Sandy, repeatedly reminded Rachel. He was divorced and, also according to Sandy, husband material going to waste. "She can start tomorrow."

"She can?" Phil grinned. "That's great. Has she had any experience in this type of work?"

Rachel nodded. "Oh yes. And she can drive the loader and the truck."

"Really?" Phil's grin widened. "My god! She looks like that and she knows how to drive a truck? She could be the find of the century."

Rachel glanced at Phil again. He didn't usually make

sexist comments. Did he fancy Quinn Farrelly? Why wouldn't he? she asked herself wryly. Quinn *was* striking. Tall. Attractive. She radiated a healthy physical fitness. And a sensuality that even Rachel was aware of.

Something unidentifiable shifted inside her, a feeling she refused to examine, or admit she'd felt before, and she berated herself. It was none of her business who Phil took a fancy to. Or Quinn Farrelly either.

Rachel pulled herself together and made herself laugh. "Looks like that and can drive a truck too? Was that a sexist remark, Phil Stevens? Why can't a woman be attractive and drive heavy machinery?"

Phil held up his hands in surrender. "Nothing sexist intended, I swear. You know what I mean."

Rachel suspected she did. More than he could know. But she wasn't about to let herself explore her own motives now, any more than she'd allowed herself to all those years ago.

"Let's hope this time we've got the right person." Phil was saying. "After that last yobbo, I'm afraid to trust my own judgment."

"I know the feeling," Rachel conceded. "Anyway, Quinn also has some experience landscaping so, at a pinch, she'll be able to help Ken out."

Phil put his hands on his hips. "She sounds too good to be true. But we're desperate, aren't we? I don't think we should look a gift horse in the mouth. What do you say?"

Rachel hesitated. Should she tell Phil about Quinn's prison record? It was common knowledge around here after all. But he would have been in the Navy when it all happened, and if anyone had told him about it he'd obviously forgotten. Rachel remained silent. It was Quinn's business. She'd paid for her mistake, and that was it as far as Rachel was concerned.

"You know, I don't think we should let her go work with

Ken though," Phil said, and Rachel raised her eyebrows in surprise. "What happens if he wants to keep her? We'd be right back where we started."

Rachel chuckled. "You mean we should do an I'm-all-right-Jack! and keep her to ourselves?"

"Exactly." Phil said with mock seriousness. "Better keep her for the Garden Center only."

They laughed and both turned as Quinn joined them. Quinn's narrowed gaze went from one to the other. Rachel wondered what the other woman was thinking, but she could glean nothing from her expression.

"I was just telling Phil we'd found a new staff member at last," Rachel said quickly. She turned back to Phil. "And actually, Quinn has a nephew who's looking for a job. She's going to ask him if he's interested in working with Ken."

"Is he as experienced with heavy machinery as you are?" Phil asked easily, and Quinn seemed to relax.

"Well, he's young, but I think he'd like the physical work."

A customer claimed Phil's attention, and he hurried off to attend to him.

"Finished all the paperwork?"

Quinn nodded. "I left it on your desk."

"Great. Come on then, I'll show you around." Rachel led the way, pointing out the various sections in the plant nursery, unaware of the sparkle in her eyes as she warmed to her subject.

She had basically talked Rob into starting the business. While her husband had been far more knowledgeable about horticulture than Rachel was back then, he had needed someone to organize the business side, to encourage him and keep him motivated. It wasn't until he was killed that Rachel realized how much of her energy had gone into that.

Once Rachel had showed Quinn the layout of the garden center, they moved through the gate into the landscaping supplies area.

A rugged man leaned against the bonnet of a battered

utility, a misshapen roll-your-own hanging from his lips. He straightened as Rachel and Quinn approached.

"Jeez, Old Dave is moving faster these days. I expected I'd have to wait half an hour." He grinned toothily and handed Rachel a docket. "Two meters of number eight, Thanks, Rach. You going to load me, love?" He roared with laughter at what he considered a huge joke.

Rachel grinned. "You know that beast of a machine hates me, Jock." She turned to Quinn. "They all think it's excruciatingly funny when I climb aboard that monster. All because I had one small accident way back when we first opened."

"One small accident, was it?" Jock laughed again. "It was touch-and-go as to whether the insurance company was going to write Mick's ute off."

"Well, Rachel, here's a chance to kill two birds with one stone," Quinn put in. "I'll load the truck, and you won't have to do it. And you can check my credentials at the same time." She held out her hand. "Got the keys?"

Rachel pulled her keys from her pocket, picked out the one that operated the loader, and handed it to Quinn. "Go to it."

"Heaven save us from women drivers," appealed Jock as Quinn strode over to the loader and swung herself up into the cabin.

They watched as the loader roared to life. Quinn expertly dug the bucket into the gravel, backed away, and headed over to the truck.

"Who's that?" Jock asked over the roar of the engine.

"Our new staff member, Quinn Farrelly."

Jock turned to look at Rachel, his eyes screwed up as smoke wafted upward from his cigarette. "Will Farrelly's kid? The one that was in the slammer?"

Rachel nodded as Quinn emptied the bucket of gravel onto the truck, barely spilling a pebble.

"How long's she been out?" Jock asked as Quinn settled the load expertly with the lip of the bucket.

"About seven years I think," Rachel replied as Quinn parked the loader and switched off the engine.

Jock looked at the load on his ute, glanced across at Quinn, and silently passed Rachel the docket for her signature. He muttered noncommittally, climbed back into his truck, and drove away.

Quinn walked back to Rachel and grinned as she handed Rachel back the key. "So. Did I pass?"

"With flying colors. You left Jock speechless," she added dryly.

Quinn pulled a face. "No mean feat, if I remember rightly. Jock worked with my father and Johnno years ago."

They walked back to the office.

"Don't forget to stop by the supplier and order your uniforms," Rachel reminded Quinn.

"Sure. And what time do you want me to start in the morning?" she asked.

"Eight-thirty. We have a roster, so I'll organize a new one by then so you'll know when your time off is. Oh, and we're flexible about that too, within reason."

"Fine. Well." Quinn inclined her head. "I'll see you in the morning."

"Yes. Welcome aboard." Rachel smiled. "I'm looking forward to working with you."

"Me too." Quinn smiled again and turned and walked away.

Rachel stood watching her, hoping desperately that she hadn't made a mistake. And Quinn's prison record was the furthermost thing from her mind.

Chapter Six

Rachel drove toward the Garden Center, humming to a sixties tune on the car radio. She'd just dropped by the job site to see how Ken was faring with his new offsider, and Rachel could see he was really pleased with Quinn's young nephew. Ken had told Rachel as long as the weather stayed fine, and allowing for the Christmas–New Year break, he should have caught up with their jobs by the middle of January.

And Ken had just discovered that young Kerrod had worked for a paving specialist during his last school vacation. Ken assured Rachel that the young man was so proficient they would be finished with their present job a week ahead of time.

It seemed she had made the right decision giving Kerrod

Farrelly a chance. He was working well with Ken, just as Quinn was working out fine at the Gardening Center.

Rachel smiled. Only yesterday Old Dave, usually taciturn, had remarked that he didn't know what he'd done without Quinn's help in the supplies section. And Phil was constantly singing Quinn's praises.

Rachel's smile faded a little. The only shadow over the whole thing was her cousin, Colleen's, attitude the day before at their bridge club meeting. And Colleen's disturbing bombshell.

Their fortnightly card game had been held at Colleen's house yesterday, and Rachel had arrived early for the first time in ages.

"What's this?" Colleen had feigned enormous amazement. "Rachel's here before we've dealt the cards. I don't believe it."

Rachel glanced at her wristwatch. "I'm only five minutes early. Hardly worth mentioning."

"Just the fact that you're early is surprise enough," Colleen remarked.

"Now don't give me a hard time, Col," Rachel protested lightly. "You know I haven't meant to be late. It was just work."

"But not today for our last meeting," Sandy said cheerfully. "And a very good way to end the old year."

"Right." Rachel smiled. "And another good way to end the year is to be able to say I'm pretty well caught up with my paperwork, mainly because my staff problems have been solved."

"You found someone at last?" asked Rhonda as Rachel sat down at the card table. "That's great. When did this happen?"

"The day after our last bridge game actually. Phil had set up an interview and it went well, and so" — Rachel shrugged — "she started the next day. She's worked in the business before and, what's more, she can drive that wretched loader."

Sandy raised her eyebrows. "She can?"

"You mean it's a woman?" Colleen put in, and Rhonda chuckled.

"Now, let's all follow the clues. She's not a man, so she must be a woman."

They all laughed.

"Very funny." Colleen pulled a face at Rhonda. "What I meant was that I was surprised you'd hired a woman, Rachel. Most women wouldn't like that kind of work."

"Most women who? Or is it whom? Whatever. *I* happen to like it," said Rachel. "And exactly what kind of work are we talking about here?"

"I know you like it, Rachel, but I just meant . . . Oh, for heaven's sake, I don't know what I meant now. Let's move on. Who is she? Does she live around here? How old is she? And do we know her?"

"And don't forget what size underwear does she wear?" quipped Sandy. "You're a typical teacher, Colleen. Questions. Questions. How about letting Rachel tell us the story?"

"Because Rachel needs prompting, that's why." Colleen replied. "You know getting gossip out of Rachel is like pulling teeth."

"It's hardly gossip, Colleen," Sandy began, but her sister quelled her with a look.

"Better unburden yourself, Rachel," suggested Rhonda, "or we'll never get our game started."

"Well." Rachel paused, suddenly a little reluctant to mention Quinn Farrelly.

"What did I tell you?" Colleen appealed, hunching her shoulders and putting her hands out, palms up. "It's like pulling teeth."

"Give her a go, Colleen," Sandy admonished and looked back expectantly at Rachel.

"Actually," Rachel began again. "You do all know her. She

was born here, but she's been . . ." Rachel paused once more. "She's been away for years, and she's just come home." Rachel swallowed.

Colleen shook her head at Rachel. "And?"

"And it's Quinn Farrelly."

For once the others were speechless.

"We did hear she'd come home," Sandy said carefully. "I remember we were talking about it at our last meeting."

"She's been away?" Colleen guffawed. "Only you would put it that way, Rachel. Quinn Farrelly's been away in prison, that's what."

"I know, Colleen," Rachel said quickly. "But she did her time and she's, well, she's trying to get on with her life."

"And I'll bet young Mark Herron would have liked to have got on with his life, too, if Quinn Farrelly hadn't killed him." Colleen put on her glasses and began shuffling the cards.

Sandy rolled her eyes at Rachel. "Now be fair, Colleen. Any one of the others could have been as responsible for what happened as Quinn was. Everyone agreed on that at the time."

Colleen sighed loudly. "Okay. Point taken. And I guess you're right," she acknowledged reluctantly. "It just seemed to me as though Quinn Farrelly's life was heading in the direction of disaster from the moment she was born."

"I wonder what Laurel Greenwood thinks about Quinn Farrelly coming home." Rhonda picked up the cards Colleen had dealt. "She'd hardly want to be reminded of all that, especially now that Mike's thinking of going into federal politics. They wouldn't want any blatant reminders of any of Laurel's indiscretions."

"Indiscretions? You wouldn't have to look far," Colleen exclaimed derisively. "Now there was another little troublemaker."

"Laurel was supposed to be Quinn's best friend." Sandy shook her head. "Sad, really. I never could understand why she didn't even show her face in court back then. She didn't, did she, Rachel?" Sandy turned to her cousin.

"No. No, she didn't." Rachel frowned. "But she was still in the hospital, and they had her statement, of course."

"Laurel's poor long-suffering parents must have been experts at getting that little villain out of scrapes," stated Colleen. "I heard they made sure Laurel stayed safely in the hospital too. As I remember, she wasn't that badly injured."

"Well, it was all irrelevant anyway," said Rachel. "Once Quinn pleaded guilty."

"So what's Quinn Farrelly like now?" Rhonda asked.

Rachel shrugged, schooling her expression. "She looks the same. But older, of course. She looks well and fit."

"She was attractive, I'll give you that." Colleen frowned. "It must have been, what did we say? Twelve years ago? She can't have been in jail for all that time. Was she?"

"No. She's been working interstate for quite a while. Then she said she decided to come home."

Colleen frowned as she sorted the cards in her hand. "Why come back now? Why not when her mother died? Sounds funny to me."

Rachel remained silent, and Colleen turned to peer at her over the top of her glasses.

"I'm concerned, Rachel."

"What about?"

"About you hiring Quinn Farrelly. About the whole thing."

"I really don't see why," Rachel said quickly. "She has wonderful references and, believe me, I can't complain about the way she works."

"Phil's a sensible guy. What does he think about her?" asked Sandy.

"I know he agrees with me," Rachel told her, feeling irrationally irritated that Sandy should think Phil's opinion was worth more than her own.

"The question is, has this particular leopard changed its

spots?" Colleen exclaimed ominously. "As I said before, trouble has followed Quinn Farrelly all her life."

"She's done her time, Colleen," Rachel reminded her cousin. "I think she should be given the chance to make a fresh start, if not for Quinn herself then for the sake of her daughter."

There was another moment of shocked silence.

"Quinn Farrelly has a child?" Colleen asked in amazement.

"Her name's Katie, and she's about five years old I think."

"Well, who would have thought it?" said Sandy. "And have you met her husband, Rachel?"

"She said she and the little girl's father weren't together any more."

"Oh dear." Sandy shook her head. "Quinn Farrelly with a family. It's sort of hard to imagine. I mean, I only remember her as a teenaged tearaway, but I guess she must be about thirty years old now. And we all had families before we were thirty, so when you look at it that way I don't know why I should be so surprised."

"Thirty or not, I'm surprised," said Colleen. "Quinn Farrelly's past aside, I always thought she batted for the other team."

Chapter Seven

Rachel's throat went dry, and she could feel heat color her face as her nerve endings prickled to attention.

"What other team?" asked Sandy innocently, and her sister turned to stare at her.

"I can't believe we're related. There must have been a mix-up at the hospital when you were born."

"We have the same features and coloring," Sandy began as Rhonda giggled.

"Honestly, Sandy," Colleen continued, "I sometimes wonder if you inhabit the same planet as the rest of us. Just tell me you know what a lesbian is."

"Of course I know what a —" Sandy's eyes grew round

and her voice dropped to a whisper. "You mean Quinn Farrelly is a lesbian?"

"That's what was whispered at the time," Colleen told her, mimicking her sister.

"Did you know that, Rachel?" Sandy asked, and Rachel swallowed.

"No. I didn't."

"See, Colleen. Rachel didn't know either."

"Rachel's almost as naive as you are, Sandy. But getting back to Quinn Farrelly, all I'm saying is, there was a story going around after one of the school socials."

"How could she be a lesbian?" Sandy asked. "She was going out with, what's his name? The guy who lost his leg?"

"The Kingston kid. Graham, I think it was," said Colleen. "So what? She was also always with Laurel Lawson. Sorry, Laurel Greenwood."

"Quinn and Laurel?" Sandy repeated in astonishment.

Rachel was just as amazed as Sandy was. She could barely take it in. Where did Colleen hear all this gossip?

"Wow!" exclaimed Rhonda. "No one told me any of this, so I didn't know either."

"I think Colleen's making it up to tease us," suggested Sandy, watching her sister for a change of expression.

Colleen shrugged. "It's just too easy to tease you, Sandy. But no, I'm not making this up, and I'm not having a go at you this time. Someone told me once one of the teachers had caught Quinn and Laurel together and that they were acting like more than friends."

Sandy scoffed at her sister. "Well, it all sounds pretty feeble to me. Laurel married Mike Greenwood not long after Quinn went to jail, and they've got three kids. Now Rachel tells us Quinn has a child too. I think you're wrong, Colleen."

"A lot of gay people get married," Colleen began, and Rhonda held up her hand.

"Now that discussion could take all afternoon. And as

intriguing as it sounds, gossiping is not the reason we're here. Why don't we get this game of bridge on the road?"

"Yes," agreed Rachel quickly. "It is our last game before Christmas. We won't be playing again until next year."

Rachel had turned her concentration to the game as they began to play, but one small part of her mind stayed on Quinn Farrelly and the enticing, terrifying questions Colleen's insinuations had aroused.

Now, driving to work, Rachel frowned as she thought about what Colleen had said about Quinn. As if she hadn't been thinking about it all night, she chastised herself irritatedly.

Looking back, Rachel knew Quinn and Laurel had been best friends in primary school and all through high school. They'd been inseparable.

But hadn't everyone had a best friend? she rationalized. Her best friend had been Janey Watson. They'd both become teachers, and they'd studied together, partied together.

Then Janey had been posted to a school in north Queensland, and they'd only seen each other when Janey came home for the holidays. Three years later Janey married a local police constable, and ever since, they'd moved around the state as her husband was transferred with his job. Rachel and Janey exchanged letters, phoned each other occasionally, and caught up with each other when Janey visited her parents every second year.

Yes, everyone had a best friend. And Laurel was Quinn's. That's all it had been, she told herself firmly.

But if Quinn was a lesbian . . . Rachel swallowed as a heady heat flared inside her. She drew a deep breath as her heart pounded erratically in her throat.

Would it make any difference if Quinn Farrelly was a lesbian? Rachel could hardly broach the subject with the other woman. She knew she wouldn't have the courage to do it.

Rachel pulled into the parking lot and climbed out of the

car. She had to put the whole idea out of her mind. Resolutely, she walked through the open gate to find Quinn and Phil standing together by the counter.

They each held a hot mug of coffee in one hand and one of Phil's mouth-watering muffins in the other. And after her unnerving thoughts about Quinn on the drive to work, Rachel found she could barely meet Quinn's gaze.

On the counter, waiting for her arrival, were Rachel's mug and a muffin, and Rachel was sure her tummy growled as the delicious aroma of the freshly brewed coffee teased her nostrils.

"Morning," Quinn and Phil said together as Rachel reached for her coffee.

She took a sip and sighed. "Ahh! That is absolute ambrosia."

Phil grinned. "And notice I'm not saying anything about skipping the most important meal of the day."

"For your information, Phil Stevens, I did have breakfast. And apart from that, do I look like I miss any meals, let alone the most important ones?" Rachel noticed that Quinn and Phil were both letting their gazes move over her. She picked up the muffin and bit into it to disguise her flush of discomposure. "Apple and cinnamon," she said inanely, and Phil's grin widened.

"I was just telling Phil that anyone who can make coffee and muffins as good as these would be definite marriage material." Quinn laughed and winked at Phil.

Rachel watched them over the rim of her coffee mug, sensing a hint of a shared joke in the look that passed between them. Was there something between Quinn and Phil? Admittedly Quinn had only been working here for two weeks, but if they were attracted to each other . . . Rachel found she didn't want to continue that particular thought. For some reason it unsettled her.

Then Colleen's words returned. *Quinn bats for the other team.*

"And I told Quinn," Phil was replying, "that I live in hope."

"In hope?" Rachel drew her whirling thoughts back to the conversation.

"That someone, the right someone, that is, will make an honest man of me," he said lightly and, picking up Quinn's empty coffee mug, walked over to the office.

Rachel stole a glance at Quinn. She was looking after Phil, a small smile playing around the corners of her mouth. A twinge of some sharp emotion Rachel refused to acknowledge was jealousy jabbed inside her, and she pretended an interest in her coffee in case Quinn should read her thoughts in her eyes.

"He's a nice guy," said Quinn. "It's a wonder someone hasn't snapped him up, isn't it?"

"Yes." Rachel agreed carefully. "He was married and divorced between when he left to join the Navy and before he came home. Is he . . .?" Rachel paused, knowing she was gossiping but unable to stop herself continuing. "Did he say he was interested in anyone in particular?"

"Not exactly." Quinn began tidying the counter, her eyes not meeting Rachel's. "But I get the impression there is someone."

"Oh." Rachel considered this information. Obviously Sandy wasn't aware of it, or she would have mentioned it to Rachel. Phil and Rachel only met socially at occasional family gatherings and, although they chatted at work, they both seemed to steer clear of any personal subjects. Rachel had preferred it that way.

She slid another glance at Quinn to find Quinn now watching her contemplatively. "Well." Rachel made herself laugh. "As you said, he is a nice guy and, as a very indifferent cook myself, anyone's cooking skills seem like an added advantage to me."

Quinn laughed too. "I know what you mean. I'm okay with the plain stuff, but I'd freak out if I had to do something exotic. So, to change the subject of our failings, how was your bridge game yesterday?"

"Oh. Fine. And speaking of failings —"

"You mean you didn't win?"

"No." Rachel grimaced ruefully. "I couldn't seem to concentrate and was dutifully admonished by my cousin Colleen."

"As in your cousin Colleen, the teacher?"

Rachel nodded. "She only teaches part time now."

Quinn shook her head. "I remember her. She could be fierce."

"That about sums Colleen up." Rachel agreed with a laugh. "If they didn't look alike, you'd never suspect Colleen and Sandy were sisters. They're about exact opposites."

"And you'd never know you were her cousin either," Quinn said softly.

Rachel's gaze met Quinn's, and any light quip Rachel might have made died on her lips as the air between them seemed to grow heavy with a strange, almost charged, uneasiness. A frisson of excitement clutched at Rachel's stomach, and she couldn't seem to focus on anything apart from the curve of Quinn's mouth, her full lips, the raised lighter ridge that delineated them.

A soft moan bubbled up inside her, but if the sound escaped it was thankfully drowned by the rumble of a small truck turning into the Supply Center.

Quinn moved, taking a step away, and then paused, looking back at Rachel. She opened her mouth to say something and hesitated again. "Seems like our workday has begun," she said lightly enough as she continued on her way.

But Rachel was sure that wasn't what Quinn had first intended to say. She took a gulp of her now cooled coffee and made herself walk toward the office.

~ ~ ~ ~ ~

46

With Christmas drawing closer, the pace at work intensified. They were rushed with Christmas orders for live trees, for Christmas gifts, and for hurried garden makeovers for the festive season. Rachel fell into bed exhausted each night with little time to reflect on anything.

As usual Rachel and the children spent Christmas Eve with Rose and Charlie at the farm. On Christmas Day they returned to share Christmas lunch with Rachel's mother, her aunt, and Colleen and Sandy's families at Colleen's large old home opposite Rachel's mother's house.

The Garden and Landscaping Center was open for a few days between Christmas and New Year but, compared to their pre-Christmas rush, business was much slower, enabling them to restock and do some much needed maintenance. It was almost closing time and, with the Garden Center empty of customers, Phil brought up the subject of what they were all intending to do for New Year's Eve.

Phil told them he would be partying at Steve and Sandy's, and Quinn said she had been invited to go along with Johnno and Josie to a work party. However, she said she wasn't keen on keeping Katie out so late.

Rachel had promised her children she'd take them into the city to Southbank to watch the fireworks.

"They have an early display for families with young children, so I decided that would suit us very well," Rachel told them.

"Sounds far more sensible," Phil said. "That's what I'd do if I had kids. Unfortunately, I'll probably end up with a hangover and spend New Year's Day deciding I'm too old and promising whoever that I won't repeat the same mistakes next New Year's Eve."

"The fireworks sound wonderful. I" — Quinn paused slightly — "I don't suppose you'd consider having company? I mean, would you mind if Katie and I tagged along with you?"

"Of course I don't mind," Rachel assured her. "It would be great to have your company. And I'd love to meet Katie."

"Sure we wouldn't be in the way?"

"Of course not. We'd be pleased to have you and Katie come with us." Rachel felt a thrill of elation she knew far outweighed what she should be feeling at the thought of spending an evening with Quinn. "It should be a good night," she added hurriedly. "The only drawback I see will be finding a car park. I guess the most sensible thing to do would be to go in the one car, so perhaps we could collect you and Katie."

"Why don't you go in on the train?" Phil suggested. "I read something in the paper just yesterday about public transport being the answer to the stress of driving into the city and parking with the other couple of hundred thousand they expect in there. The train takes you right to Southbank, and they're even putting on extra services especially for New Year."

Rachel and Quinn looked at each other.

"I know Adam would really enjoy the train ride. What do you think, Quinn?"

Quinn nodded. "I can't remember when I last took a ride on a train. Sounds like fun. What say Katie and I pick you up, and then you won't have to leave your car at the station? Not even a New Year's Eve reveler is going to try to steal my Gemini. I'd have to pay them to take it."

They made arrangements about times, and it was all set. Rachel found herself smiling all the way home. Suddenly she was looking forward to New Year's Eve even more. It was a, well, comfortable way to get to know Quinn again, she rationalized.

Chapter Eight

The three children were pressed against the glass window, pointing at the lights of houses as the train flashed past. Rachel sat across from Quinn, wishing she could be as relaxed as the other woman so obviously was.

Quinn sat back in her seat in a pose Rachel now associated with her, one jean-clad leg crossed casually over the other, her sneaker-clad foot moving slightly with the sway of the train. Quinn's arm rested along the back of the seat, her hand lightly holding the belt of Katie's shorts, steadying the child as she knelt beside the window.

"Katie will be okay," said Fliss as she slipped onto the seat between Quinn and the little girl. "I'll hold her for you."

Ten-year-old Fliss had inherited her father's height and

her mother's fair coloring. Adam, Rachel felt, took after her father's family and had a stockier build and dark hair.

Quinn smiled at Fliss and turned back to Rachel. "The fireworks were fantastic, weren't they?"

"The best I've seen," Rachel agreed, wishing she had the nerve to add what she was really thinking. *And they were all the more fantastic because you were there with us.*

Rachel silently chastised herself. She had to keep the situation light, social. Any thoughts of anything else were . . . She had to stop this right now. It was just a carryover from her adolescent fantasies, she told herself.

But the problem was, this thing she had for Quinn, had always had for Quinn, didn't feel like some infantile teenage crush. If it ever had. That's what had scared her years ago. However, what was relevant, and always had been relevant, was the fact that she knew she couldn't act on any of it.

"So, have you decided to make any New Year's resolutions?" Quinn asked, and Rachel pulled her tortured thoughts into order.

"New Year resolutions? I usually do make some. Of course, keeping them is another thing altogether." Rachel pretended to give the question grave thought. *To stop trying to revive old dreams about you.* What would Quinn say if Rachel voiced such outrageous thoughts? "I guess I'll make the same one I made last year. To be more organized."

"You seem pretty organized to me," Quinn said.

Rachel grimaced. "It's all an illusion, believe me."

"Daddy used to say Mum ran around like a chook with its head cut off," Fliss told Quinn, and Quinn raised her eyebrows.

"The implication was that I was a trifle disorganized," Rachel said without rancor, knowing it had been partly true. Since she'd been on her own she rather thought she'd learned the hard way that she had to have some semblance of organization or everything fell apart.

"Well, I still stick by what I said. Running the business. Organizing your home and family. That mustn't be easy. You seem to manage really well."

Rachel laughed softly. "Sometimes I feel like it's all teetering like a house of cards. One slight tremor and the whole thing will collapse."

She looked across the small space at Quinn and then quickly away again, suspecting that she could drown in those clear gray eyes. "What about you? Any resolutions of your own?"

Quinn shrugged. "Not a resolution as such, but I do know I have to find somewhere for Katie and me to live. We've been with Johnno and Josie since we returned, and I only intended staying for a couple of weeks. I want to be settled before Katie has to start school at the end of the month."

Quinn sat forward, rested her elbows on her knees, and Rachel felt a warm heat flow through her body at Quinn's nearness. She swallowed, suppressing the urge to reach out, run her fingers along the line of Quinn's jaw, feel the softness of her lips.

This was getting totally out of hand. She had to keep reminding herself about the difference between fantasy and reality.

She was a married woman, a mother with the responsibility of raising two children, the widow of a well-liked man who had spent his whole life in this district. She was a business entity in her own right. There was no way she could allow these feelings to intrude on any part of her life. But, oh how Rachel wanted to.

"Not that Johnno has asked us to leave," Quinn was continuing. "Their house is fairly spacious. But Katie and I are in Kerrod's room, and he has to share with his brother, so that's not really fair on him. Apart from that, I like to be independent."

Rachel nodded. And suddenly a thought occurred to her, a

wild, totally inappropriate idea that made her heartbeats fall all over themselves. "What" — she swallowed again — "what will you be looking for? A house?"

"Probably." Quinn frowned slightly. "I'd like a bit of a garden for Katie. Then again, I guess a flat or a unit would be more practical." She grimaced. "The bottom line would be the price. Rents these days aren't cheap. They're much higher than I expected them to be."

"Why can't Quinn and Katie have our flat, Mum?" asked Fliss, and both women turned to the young girl. "Well, you said the other day you were going to rent it out again, now that Tom and Bazza have left."

Out of the mouths of babes, Rachel thought to herself. Her daughter had casually voiced Rachel's own idea before Rachel could formulate a spontaneous sounding way to offer Quinn their unit.

But would it be sensible to have Quinn Farrelly so close? Rachel knew the answer to that, but she pushed it away.

"I, we do have a unit at our place," Rachel began. "It's not big, but it's self-contained. Just one bedroom and an open plan living-dining-kitchen area. The bedroom's quite big, though."

"And you rent it out?" Quinn asked.

"Yes. Usually to a couple of students attending the college. We've rented it to students ever since my mother-in-law remarried and moved out to the farm." She told Quinn how much she usually charged for the unit. "Actually, we, that is, Rob and I, built it for his mother when she decided her house was too big for her. There's a connecting door into the main house, but it's a double door and we just keep it locked when it's rented out. So it's quite private. And there's a carport for your car."

"Now that's a must." Quinn laughed easily. "I'm sure the Gemini wouldn't know itself if it got to have its own garage."

Rachel laughed too.

"I think you should trade the Gemini in," suggested Adam

52

seriously. "Otherwise no one will give you even ten dollars for it."

"I doubt they'd give me that now," Quinn told him. "But," she sighed, "there's no way we'll be able to afford a new car for a while yet."

"Maybe Grandpa Charlie could look at it." Adam beamed. "Gran says he's a whiz with machinery."

"I think maybe the Gemini needs a miracle." Quinn chuckled and then turned back to Rachel. "But I would like to have a look at the unit. If it's all right with you."

"Of course. Whenever you'd like."

"Here's our station, Mum," said Adam, standing up, and they all filed out to leave the train.

"Taking the train was the best idea," Rachel said as the Gemini coughed up the hill toward Rachel's place. "Thanks for suggesting it."

"No problem." Quinn dropped down a gear, and the car seemed to heave a sigh of relief as it crested the rise. Quinn drew to a halt in front of the house.

Now that they were home Rachel was loath to have the evening finally over. It was the best New Year's Eve she'd spent in, well, for as long as she could remember.

Rob had always been in a party mood on New Year's Eve and dragged them to as many parties as he could manage. Rachel had had to drive so Rob could enjoy a drink, and he'd usually been asleep in the car before they finally reached home. The next morning they'd had to tiptoe around the house because of his hangover.

"Would you like to come in and look at the unit now?" Rachel asked quickly. "Unless it's too late."

Quinn glanced at the wristwatch on her arm, her eyes narrowing in the dull interior light of the car. "No. It's okay. If it's not inconvenient for you."

"It's a good opportunity." Rachel climbed from the car.

"Mum, I can't get out," said Adam from the back, and Rachel leaned inside to help him untangle his seat belt.

"There's a lot to be said for the retractable numbers," Quinn said wryly as she climbed in the other side and deftly undid Adam's belt. "You weren't holding your mouth right, mate," she said and Adam giggled as he scrambled out of the car.

They walked up the front path, Fliss giving Katie a piggyback ride, setting her down on the step. "That's the unit on that side of the house," she told Quinn.

"It has its own driveway, and the carport's around in back," Rachel said as she unlocked the door to the house. She switched on the light in the foyer, and they went inside.

"This is nice," Quinn said as she looked around.

"The door to the unit's through here," said Adam, running across to get to the door before his sister. He pulled open the door and then pushed the matching door into the unit.

"I want to show Quinn and Katie," said Fliss, giving her brother a shove. "I thought of it first."

"Quit it, you two." Rachel admonished them. "Otherwise Quinn will think twice about living next door to two precocious brats." She pulled a face at Quinn. "As I said, the door's usually locked, so you'd have your privacy. And it's well insulated so you wouldn't have to listen to me screaming at these two." She leaned around the corner and flicked on the light before standing back to let Quinn go inside.

Quinn walked through to the unit, and they all followed her.

"The bedroom's through here." Fliss opened the door with a flourish. "It's got its own bathroom, too."

"You're right," Quinn said. "The bedroom's quite large. And the furniture comes with it?"

The room held two single beds, two chests of drawers, and one entire wall of built-in cupboards.

"Yes. As is. But we can always store the furniture if you have your own."

"No. I don't. Not much anyway. That's been the problem.

Finding the rental bond and then having to buy furniture. We sold off our other stuff before we came home."

"And this is the bathroom." Adam flicked on the light. "It's as big as ours."

The three children followed Quinn into the bathroom, and Rachel stood at the door. "Maybe not so big with the whole football team crowding inside," she said wryly.

Quinn laughed. "It's big enough."

They retraced their steps and went into the small kitchenette.

"Look, Mummy. It has a fridge, too," exclaimed Katie.

"And a microwave," added Fliss, opening and shutting the door like a hopeful real estate agent.

"And a washing machine," said Quinn softly as she looked into the small laundry.

"That's old, but it works well," Rachel told her. "You can share our clothesline or use the one under the carport. The carport's outside the back door there, by the way. Rose got Rob to build that after a hailstorm dented her car." She chuckled. "A bit like closing the stable door after the horse has bolted. But we were ready for the next big storm. We had a spate of bad ones a few years ago."

"And Katie can use our garden any time," said Fliss. "And the pool."

"You have a pool?" Katie clapped her small hands. "I love swimming."

"We wouldn't impose on you," Quinn began. "I mean, I'd love to take the flat. And Katie and I wouldn't trouble you."

"It's no trouble." Rachel felt as though a full choir were singing "Hallelujah" inside her. While a small part of her chided herself, reminded her that this was totally insane. Having Quinn so close was . . .

"It's great. So when can we move in?" Quinn said with a smile.

"Tomorrow?" suggested Katie eagerly, and Rachel laughed.

"If you want to. I had it professionally cleaned when the boys left, so it should only need dusting."

"I could bring some stuff around tomorrow or Monday." Quinn flushed a little. "It would be great to get settled before going back to work on Tuesday. Would that be okay?"

"Fine." Rachel smiled.

"Excellent," said Fliss as Adam danced up and down.

"You'll be living with us. You'll be living with us," he yelled excitedly.

"They'll change their minds if you continue making so much noise," Rachel reprimanded him.

"Boys can be a drag sometimes," Fliss told Katie as they went back into the main house.

"So can girls," Adam retorted and turned to his mother. "I'm hot, Mum. Can we have a swim? Want to come for a swim, Katie?"

"We'd better be getting off home," Quinn said quickly. "We don't want to outstay our welcome."

"Oh, Mummy," Katie appealed. "Can't we have a swim first?"

"We didn't bring our swimsuits." Quinn glanced apologetically at Rachel.

"We've got spare suits," Fliss said, and Rachel laughed.

"There's nothing like a swim to cool you down on a hot summer night," Rachel said softly and felt her throat constrict on the words. And was she imagining the dull flush that colored Quinn's cheeks? Rachel's breath caught somewhere in her chest, and she coughed slightly.

Chapter Nine

Of course she'd imagined it, she told herself brutally. She'd better have imagined it, she added ruthlessly, because if she hadn't, well . . . It had all been too hard twelve years ago. And it was even harder now.

"We've just sorted through our clothes, so we have stacks of stuff for you to choose from," Fliss was saying as they moved back into the main house.

"Mum's going to give them to Saint Vinnie's because we don't wear them any more," Adam added, continuing the story.

"It was a job I'd been going to do all last year," Rachel explained to Quinn. "Finally got it done a couple of days ago." She pulled open a large storage bag.

"Here." Rachel held out a swimsuit. "This should fit you. I've sort of outgrown it."

Quinn's gray eyes moved over Rachel, making Rachel's skin prickle with nervous awareness. "I wouldn't have said you'd put on weight."

Rachel grimaced. "That's exceptionally generous of you to say, but my clothes tell me a totally different story."

"Well, what's a few pounds here or there? You look pretty good regardless."

"Of all the mothers in my class, Mum's the prettiest," Adam said, and Rachel gave him a quick hug, feeling her cheeks warm with a blush.

Quinn laughed easily. "There you go. We all can't be wrong."

"If the togs don't fit, maybe you could use a T-shirt and shorts." Even as she suggested it, Rachel's mind threw up a rather graphic picture of Quinn in a wet T-shirt, the thin material clinging to the curve of breasts and hips.

"How about these for Katie?" Fliss said as she pulled a discarded pair of swimmers of her own from the large plastic bag she was rummaging in. "Do you think they'll be too big?"

Rachel was grateful she could turn her attention to her daughter. "They should be fine. Thanks, love. Now, Quinn and Katie can use the laundry here to change, and we'll dash upstairs. Oh, there's clean towels there on the shelf. Just help yourselves."

"Thanks," said Quinn.

"Are you going to wear your new Christmas togs, Mum?" Fliss asked, and Rachel could only nod. "Gran Richardson gave them to Mum," Fliss explained to Quinn. "And they're really pretty."

"I like the color of mine," said Katie, holding up the swimmers Fliss had given her. She began to wriggle out of her shirt.

"Whoa. Where's your modesty, young lady?" Quinn said quickly, and Rachel laughed.

"Come on," she said to her two. "We'll all meet back here in a couple of minutes."

As Rachel left Quinn and Katie, she heard the little girl ask her mother what modesty was. Rachel's grin broadened.

Adam and Fliss ran down the hall to their own rooms, and Rachel went into hers. She opened the door to her walk-in closet and took her new swimsuit off the shelf.

As Fliss had informed Quinn, Rachel's mother had given the suit to her for Christmas, telling her to throw away the old one she had been wearing for years. Her mother had very good taste, Rachel acknowledged, as she held up the one-piece suit. The material was a swirl of wonderfully rich shades of blue, but Rachel knew she would have preferred a pair that didn't show so much of her generous cleavage.

When she'd said as much, after they'd opened their presents on Christmas Day, Sandy had laughingly suggested Rachel be daring for a change. Colleen had rolled her eyes exasperatedly and remarked that Rachel wouldn't know how.

Rachel pulled a face as she remembered. What would her cousin Colleen say if Rachel told her of her fantasies about Quinn Farrelly? Would that be daring enough for Colleen?

Rachel slipped out of her clothes and into the new swimsuit. She caught sight of herself in the long, mirrored door.

She didn't cut a terribly fine figure in next to nothing, she thought ruefully, making a self-derisive face at herself in the mirror. She wasn't exactly model material. She pulled at the top of the suit, settling it more comfortably over her full breasts.

Unconsciously she sucked in her tummy, only succeeding in accentuating her breasts. Since she'd had the children, her breasts, always fuller than most young women her age, had grown somewhat, well, *tired*, she decided was the best description. And tired, she told herself, was teetering on the edge of full-blown *sagging*.

She suppressed an almost hysterical giggle and then

sobered. She'd lay odds that *tired* and *sagging* would be words that wouldn't have one thing in common with Quinn's breasts.

As a teenager Quinn had always been long and lithe, the complete antithesis of Rachel. And yet Quinn had also been totally feminine. The day Rachel had inadvertently come upon her in the showers . . . Rachel stopped, her hand going to the prickle of awareness that teased at her stomach.

The memory careered back and forth in her mind with amazing clarity.

One of Rachel's jobs as a student teacher had been to assist the sports mistress. One afternoon Rachel had been counting heads as the girls came out of the sports block. They had been playing netball and had all showered before continuing on to their various classes.

Rachel's count had been one short. Quinn Farrelly, of course, the sports mistress had stated in disgust, and sent Rachel to look for Quinn. Rachel had hurried into the locker room and glanced around. A black sports bag lay on one of the benches. The door to the showers was open, and Rachel took a step inside, worried that Quinn may have fainted or been taken ill.

There was a figure inside. Quinn had finished showering and was drying herself off, her back to Rachel.

Rachel stood transfixed, unable to prevent her gaze from moving over the sleek lines of Quinn's naked body. Her wide, well-defined shoulders. Her narrow waist and slim hips. Her rounded buttocks and long, well-shaped legs. And as Quinn moved, bent forward, Rachel saw the curve of one small firm breast.

What followed was burned indelibly into Rachel's memory bank. The intervening years hadn't so much as blurred her recall. Back then a burning fire had raged over Rachel's body. She'd wanted to move closer and run away. She'd been ashamed and yet so very excited.

In those split seconds she'd wondered what Quinn would have thought if she'd turned, seen Rachel, realized Rachel was watching her. Would what she'd been thinking have been visible on her face? In her eyes? Of course it would have. And it was entirely inappropriate.

Rachel had angrily reminded herself she was a teacher, if only one of the lowly student variety, but a teacher for all that. She was in a position of trust, and Quinn was a student. My god! What could she be thinking?

Hardly daring to breathe, Rachel had backed out of the shower room. And she'd wanted to run out of the locker room, flee from the confusion that the glimpse of Quinn Farrelly's naked body had caused within her.

But she knew she couldn't go outside, face the other students like this. They'd know something was wrong. And she couldn't go outside without Quinn Farrelly either. She'd have to let Quinn know she was here.

Rachel had made herself pause, wait until her breathing was steady, until she was once more in command of herself. Then she coughed loudly.

"Quinn? Are you still here?" Her voice was almost even.

Quinn appeared in the doorway, her towel wrapped around her like a sarong. "Sure, Rach — I mean, Miss Richardson. Sorry I'm late. I slipped and the floor was all gritty. I thought it would be easier to take another shower."

"Did you, did you hurt yourself?" Rachel asked, and Quinn shook her head.

"Nah. Just a scrape." She indicated a red graze on one knee.

Rachel took a step closer and then stopped. "It looks like you've broken the skin. I think you should have the nurse put some antiseptic on it. In fact, you'd better go along now, before your next class."

"Sure." Quinn shrugged. "I'll just get dressed."

She went to step out of the towel, and Rachel quickly

turned to the door. "I'll wait outside for you." And she'd slipped out into the sunshine, the fresh air, away from the temptation of again looking at Quinn. And how it made her feel.

How many times over the years had Rachel taken out that memory, relived it, examined it, and replaced it? Rachel sighed. Well, there was one good thing. She was no longer Quinn Farrelly's teacher. No, now she was her boss, reminded a ruthless little voice inside her. Had the situation changed? It would seem not.

Impatiently Rachel grabbed up her towel and draped it concealingly over her shoulder before she left her room and hurried downstairs.

"What took you so long, Mum?" demanded Adam. "We've been waiting hours for you."

"Sorry." She flashed a quick glance at Quinn, who was smiling at the impatient children.

Rachel swallowed, deciding she had never looked as good in that old swimsuit as Quinn now did. "The suit fits okay then?" she said quickly to disguise her interest.

"Well enough." Quinn laughed.

"Let's go." Adam danced over to the door and reached up to flick on the pool lights.

Rachel opened the back door, and they all filed outside, the children running excitedly ahead.

The turquoise water glistened under the lights, coolly welcoming. Soon they were all in the water, luxuriating in its refreshing softness.

"This is fantastic," Quinn said, wiping her wet hair back from her face. "Really cools your body temperature down."

"Watch me swim, Mummy." Katie pushed herself away from the side of the pool, and Rachel started in concern.

"She's okay," Quinn reassured Rachel quickly. "She swims well. I had her taught when she was a baby."

Rachel watched as the child moved through the water. "She's really good."

Quinn smiled, obviously pleased.

"She reminds me of you," Rachel added softly, and Quinn raised her eyebrows.

"Does she?"

"You were always the star swimmer on the school team. Katie has your style."

Quinn looked back at her daughter. "The guy who taught her to swim said she was a natural. Maybe I'll get her coaching when she gets older." She leaned back against the side of the pool. "In a couple of years she can decide if she's interested or not. I just don't want to be one of those mothers who force their kids to perform. You know, overachieving parents."

Rachel nodded. "I think it's important kids enjoy what they're doing. I can't see any point in pressuring them." Rachel turned back to look at Quinn.

"Me neither." Quinn was watching her daughter, her elbows resting on the side of the pool, her wet bathing suit clinging to the contours of her body.

And suddenly Rachel found herself staring at the perfect symmetry of Quinn's broad shoulders, her long neck, firm chin. She had that smooth light olive skin that always looked slightly tanned, and Rachel could see a faint, fine line on her muscular arms where the sun had darkened her skin to her shirt line.

The water gleamed on her shoulders, rivulets running downward to disappear between her small breasts. Rachel felt her cheeks flame as she realized she could see the faint outline of Quinn's nipples. She had a burning urge to lean forward, catch those droplets of water with the tip of her tongue, and then lose herself in the mystery of that forbidden cleavage. What if she was to . . .

Rachel's heartbeats accelerated, and she turned and dived into the water, away from Quinn, away from the almost irresistible temptation.

Adam blew up an inflatable beach ball, and they had an energetic and noisy game of water polo.

"Not so loud, Adam," Rachel admonished her son as she clung to the side of the pool to catch her breath. "Lucky the neighbors are all out."

"Noise is excused on New Year's Eve." Quinn laughed and threw Rachel the ball.

Rachel caught it and sank below the surface, coming up coughing and spluttering. "I wasn't ready for that," she protested.

"You have to stay alert, Mum," said Fliss. "That's what it's all about."

"No doubt," Rachel replied dryly as Quinn laughed.

"Well, guess who's got the ball. Let's get her, kids."

Rachel pushed herself away from the side of the pool, aware of the splashing behind her as she headed for the shallow end. Suddenly long arms reached out, wrapped around her waist, halted her progress. She was pulled back against a strong, contoured frame, unexpected warmth spreading over her body.

Chapter Ten

She could feel the smoothness of Quinn's legs tangled with her own, the jut of Quinn's hip, the firmness of her breasts pressed against her bare back. And Rachel dropped the ball in surprise.

"I've got it," yelled Adam, pouncing on the ball. "Another point for us. Quinn and me win."

It seemed like an hour rather than seconds before Quinn's arms released Rachel. Her feet touched the bottom, and she struggled to draw a steadying breath before she looked at Quinn.

The other woman's lips curved upward in that teasing smile that Rachel had remembered all those years. And yet Rachel was sure there was something else in Quinn's eyes, an awareness that struck a chord deep inside Rachel and made her face burn again.

"Gotcha," Quinn said easily enough, and Rachel made herself smile back.

"I think you've had more practice at this than I have."

Quinn's smile faltered just slightly. "I think you may be right," she said softly, ambiguously, as she turned back to the children.

Eventually they climbed out of the pool and returned to the house, drying off and changing back into their clothes.

Rachel suggested a drink and cookies, and the children agreed excitedly. She glanced at her kitchen clock as she crossed to the fridge to get milk for the children. She had set the kettle boiling to make some tea for herself and Quinn.

Quinn was in the living room with the children after Rachel had refused her offer of help. They'd switched on the television as the New Year's fireworks spectacular from Sydney was due to start any minute.

Rachel set the drinks on a tray and reached for the cookies, dropping one as she recalled that torrid moment in the pool when Quinn had had her arms around her. Rachel had thought she'd ignite she felt so hot. Surely Quinn must have felt it too.

Rachel paused, the biscuit barrel in her hand. Did Quinn realize just what effect her nearness had on Rachel? A tiny quiver of excitement fluttered in the pit of Rachel's stomach, grew just as suddenly and raced around inside her, only to settle and intensify. She felt damp, and her nipples hardened. For one horrifying moment she thought her legs would give way beneath her, and she put the biscuit barrel back on the counter in case it slipped from her trembling fingers.

All those years ago there had been that unsettling awareness. And now, Rachel knew without doubt she was physically attracted to Quinn Farrelly. And the thought filled her with terror. And a tumult of excitement.

No one, not even Rob, had caused such a burning need

inside her, this almost overwhelming craving to want to . . .
Rachel bit her lip. She wanted to pull Quinn into her arms,
hold her close, feel every curve of her strong body, her
nearness, her heat.

"Rachel?"

Rachel started guiltily.

Quinn was standing in the doorway. "Sure you don't need
any help?"

"Oh no. Thanks." Rachel pulled herself together. "I was
just about to put the cookies on a plate."

"Okay." Quinn frowned slightly. "It's just that the kettle
is about to whistle itself off the counter."

"Oh." Rachel reached out and flicked off the switch.
"Sorry. I must have been daydreaming."

"Sure you're not too tired for this?" Quinn had taken a
few steps into the small kitchen. "I mean, it is late and I, well,
I didn't intend staying so long. Katie and I could go on home."

"No. I'm fine," Rachel reassured her quickly. "Really. And
I do want to watch the fireworks on Sydney Harbor."

Quinn held her gaze. "Shall I take the kids' drinks in for
you?" she asked.

"That would be great." She poured the hot water into the
teapot. "How do you have your tea?"

"Black, thanks. Not too strong. With one sugar." Quinn
left with the tray of drinks, and Rachel tried to relax.

She finished making the tea and, taking a steadying
breath, she joined the others in the living room.

The children were sitting on the large beanbag chair that
Adam had dragged in from the garage, all three happily
munching on cookies. Rachel handed Quinn her tea and sat
down on the couch beside her. Luckily it was a long couch, she
told herself derisively, although not long enough. She was sure
she could feel Quinn's heat reaching her.

"You're just in time, Mum," said Adam. "The fireworks are
just starting."

Rachel picked up the remote control and turned the

volume down a little as the fireworks began to explode, bathing the beautiful harbor in starbursts of color. They sat back and enjoyed the spectacular.

Rachel left the TV on after the fireworks ended, and both she and Quinn finished their drinks. One by one the children dozed off.

"Did you watch this on TV last year?" Quinn asked softly so she didn't wake the now sleeping children. "It seems to get better each year."

Rachel agreed. "And it's amazing the way they get the fireworks to look like water cascading off the bridge."

Quinn drained her cup, and Rachel switched off the television set.

"Well, a new year dawns," she said quietly, watching the three children sleeping in the large beanbag chair.

"Do you believe in a new beginning?" Quinn asked, and Rachel turned back to her.

"I guess I do." She gave a soft laugh. "But the more cynical among us would say it is just another day."

Quinn smiled too. "Doesn't sound as good, does it?"

"Not at all. Want another cup of tea?"

"Not unless I want to stay awake until another day dawneth." She chuckled. "Too much tea has the same effect on me late at night as coffee does. Wakes me up. I'd better get Katie home. Perhaps I could ring you tomorrow before I bring some stuff over to the flat?"

"We'll be here all day. My mother and my aunt will probably be coming for lunch."

Rachel went to stand up, but Quinn had moved before she did. She reached out, took hold of Rachel's hand, and pulled her to her feet. And she didn't immediately release Rachel's hand. Rachel paused, her whole body suddenly tense as they stood together.

"Rachel, I" — Quinn looked at the floor and then back at Rachel — "I just wanted to say thank you."

"What for?" Rachel's voice sounded tight and strained, and she swallowed quickly.

"For everything. The job. The flat. For not holding my jail time against me." Quinn shrugged. "For giving me a chance, I guess."

"We all make mistakes, Quinn, large and small. Some of us just get caught out more than others. You paid for what you did, and everyone deserves a second chance."

"I don't think I'll ever pay for what I did," Quinn said softly, her thumb absently rubbing the back of Rachel's hand.

Rachel was sure Quinn was unaware she was doing it, but her touch sent tiny spirals of sensations tingling up Rachel's arm.

"Nothing will bring back a lost life," Quinn was continuing. "But I suppose all I can do is try to be the best person I can for the rest of my life."

Rachel nodded, unable to speak at the look of abject sadness on the other woman's face. Quinn slowly let go of Rachel's hand. And Rachel suddenly wanted her to take her hand again. She wanted to pull Quinn into her arms, wrap her arms around her, comfort her.

Then Quinn leaned forward, lightly, quickly kissed Rachel's cheek. "Happy New Year, Rachel," she said softly, and then she shrugged. "As I said, time to take my sleeping child and go." She walked over and lifted Katie effortlessly into her arms. "What about Adam and Fliss?"

"They're okay. I'll get them to bed after I see you off." Rachel made herself move, followed Quinn out to the car, watched her settle the drowsy child into her seat belt.

Quinn straightened. "Might see you tomorrow then if Johnno's not too exhausted from his partying. Otherwise it will be Monday. Okay?"

"Fine." Rachel smiled. "Anytime."

Quinn slid into the driver's seat and pulled away, the car stuttering as it labored along the street.

Rachel stood and watched the disappearing taillights, her hand going to her warm cheek, touching the place where Quinn's so soft lips had brushed her skin.

On Sunday Rachel's mother and her aunt came over for a late lunch. Afterward the children splashed in the pool while the three women sat in the cool under the pergola. They were reminiscing about Christmas lunch at Colleen's when the phone rang.

Rachel picked up the cordless phone she'd brought outside with her. "Rachel Weston."

"Hi, Rachel. It's Quinn Farrelly."

"Oh. Hello." Rachel felt a smile lift the corners of her mouth.

"About my big move. We've all decided it would be best if we bring my stuff over to the flat first thing in the morning, when we're fresh. That's if, in the bright light of day, you haven't had second thoughts about renting the unit to us."

"No, of course I haven't," Rachel reassured her quickly. "And you can move in whenever it suits you. I take it your brother had a good New Year?"

Quinn laughed softly, the sound flowing over Rachel, enveloping her, making her feel decidedly warm. "You got that right. They didn't get home until three A.M., so Johnno looks pretty much like a sleepwalker."

There was a muffled comment, and Quinn laughed again. "He says I'm picking on him and that Josie looks no better than he does."

"And does she?" Rachel asked.

"Sure she does. We women have to stick together."

"That we do."

"Anyway, I'll get everything packed today, and we'll head over in the morning. Not too early. If that fits in with you."

"That will be fine. We'll be home."

"All right then. Well," Quinn paused. "I'll see you tomorrow. And Rachel? Thanks again."

"That's okay. Bye." Rachel broke the connection and set the phone back on the table beside her.

"You're renting out the unit again?" asked Rachel's mother. Rachel nodded.

"As of tomorrow."

Charlotte Richardson frowned. "I'm still not in favor of you having strangers in the house, dear. You just don't know about people these days. Are they more college students?"

"Not this time." Rachel swallowed. "Actually, it's a woman and her young daughter."

"Well, that doesn't seem so bad." Rachel's aunt, her mother's sister, took a sip of her tea. "She could be company for you, Rachel. Don't you think so, Charlotte?"

Rachel's mother continued to frown. "I suppose it's better than students," she agreed reluctantly.

Adam ran from the pool and picked up his lemonade. "Was that Quinn?" he asked. Rachel nodded. "Are they coming today?"

"In the morning."

"Oh." Adam sighed loudly. "Katie could have come swimming with us if they'd come today." He took a gulp of his drink and returned to the pool. "Quinn and Katie are coming tomorrow," he shouted to his sister.

"Quinn and Katie?" Charlotte Richardson's eyes narrowed, and there was a moment's telling silence. "Is that Quinn Farrelly?"

"Yes, it is." Rachel took a drink of her own cup of tea, hoping she didn't sound as defensive as she felt.

71

"You've rented the flat to Quinn Farrelly?"

"Well, yes. She was looking for somewhere to stay, so . . ." Rachel shrugged.

"Rachel, I've been meaning to talk to you about all this since Colleen told me you'd hired that girl."

"Mum, she's thirty years old. She's hardly a girl, and she has a five-year-old daughter."

"She's still Quinn Farrelly. And having her working at the Garden Center is bad enough, but to have her in your home . . ." Charlotte shook her head. "I just don't think it's a good idea."

"She was sent to jail, Mum," Rachel said softly, aware that the children were almost within earshot. "But she's served her time. That part of her life is over."

"Rachel's right, Charlotte," said her sister. "She *has* served her time. I agree with Rachel. She's entitled to another chance," she added in a tone not unlike her daughter Sandy had used when talking about Quinn.

"We don't know what sort of criminals she mixed with in prison. Or what bad habits she picked up." Rachel's mother shook her head. "You hear such awful stories. She could rob you or, or anything."

"I'm sure she won't do anything of the kind, Mum. She has excellent references." Rachel held up her hand as her mother went to interrupt. "Which I've checked. And since she started at the Garden Center, her work's been exemplary. So? What's to worry about that?"

"I'm sure Rachel's right," said Aunt Anne.

"But why does it have to be Rachel who gives Quinn Farrelly a chance?" Charlotte pleaded.

"Mum, stop worrying." Rachel patted her mother's hand. "When you meet Quinn, you'll realize there's no need to. And Katie, her little girl, is delightful."

"Didn't Sandy say Quinn's not with the little girl's father any more?" asked Rachel's aunt.

"As far as I know they're separated. And I don't think he's involved in Katie's life."

"Oh. That's so sad. Such a pity."

"What if she starts bringing men into the house?" Rachel's mother suggested ominously.

Aunt Anne winked at Rachel. "What if she does, Charlotte? Maybe he'll have a brother who'll suit Rachel."

"Now we're getting ridiculous," said Rachel and turned to her mother. "Mum, why don't you come down to the Garden Center next week and meet Quinn, talk to her. I know it will make you feel better."

"I'll come down with you, Charlotte," said Aunt Anne. "We knew her mother. The Driscolls lived down the street from us when we were girls. Laura was a lovely young woman. No wonder Will Farrelly was smitten."

Rachel's aunt and mother went on to talk about the Farrellys, but Rachel tuned out, absently watching the children play in the pool. She wondered what her mother would say if she knew just what part Rachel's past feelings for Quinn had played in Rachel's life. And how Rachel wished Quinn could be part of her future.

The Gemini and a well-kept utility pulled up in the driveway at eight-thirty the next morning.

"It's Quinn," yelled Adam, throwing open the front door before Rachel could prevent him.

She'd have to have a talk to both children, remind them about honoring Quinn's privacy, just as they had the boys when they rented the unit.

Rachel followed the children outside, smiling as Quinn and an exuberant Katie climbed out of the car.

"The gang's all here," quipped Quinn.

"So I see."

At that moment Johnno Farrelly and a teenaged boy, who was such a carbon copy of Johnno he could only be Johnno's son, walked up to Quinn.

Quinn made the introductions. "You know Johnno, don't you, Rachel? And his younger son, Nathan. Kerrod's brother."

Johnno shook Rachel's hand. "I coached Rob's cricket team one year."

Rachel nodded as Johnno looked up at the house, his gaze settling on the open door to the unit.

"I've opened all the doors and windows, let in some fresh air."

"Great," said Quinn. She slapped Johnno on the back. "Well, brother, now for phase two of the big move."

Rachel paused. "Can I do anything to help?"

"No. We'll be fine, thanks, Rachel. I think most of it's Katie's toys. Or that's what it seems like."

As if to emphasize the point, Nathan swung a bright pink bicycle out of the back of the ute. Katie ran forward, excitedly taking hold of the bike and telling Adam and Fliss that Santa Claus had brought it for her because she'd been good all year. The three children went off around the back of the house.

Quinn, Johnno, and Nathan were busy unloading boxes. Rachel stood undecided. She felt she could hardly stand there and watch, and she didn't want to push herself forward when Quinn had declined her offer of help. She reluctantly went back into the house.

She found herself wandering around, straightening magazines and fluffing cushions, all the while listening to the sounds from next door. Eventually she went into the kitchen and heated the kettle. She set out cups and cookies on a tray and carried the tray out on the patio.

When the sounds of activity ceased, she crossed to knock on the connecting door. Quinn opened the door to her knock.

"How's it going?" Rachel asked her.

"Last box coming in now."

"I've made some tea." Rachel paused. "I thought . . . Moving's thirsty work."

"Thanks." Quinn smiled and turned to Johnno and Nathan as they set down a large box on the kitchen counter. "Rachel's made tea."

"Or you could have a cold drink if you prefer," Rachel put in.

"I wouldn't say no to a cuppa," said Johnno, and they followed Rachel through the house and out onto the back patio.

Rachel sorted out the drinks and they sat down, shaded by the pergola, a nice cool breeze drifting across the back garden.

Quinn and Nathan took cans of drink over to the children, who were playing on the wooden climbing frame, leaving Johnno and Rachel virtually alone.

"Nice pool," said Johnno as he sipped his tea.

"Especially in this hot weather," said Rachel with a smile.

"I can imagine." Johnno looked down at the cup in his hand. "The unit looks just the show for Quinn and Katie. My wife, Josie, and I appreciate that Quinn's got someone close by. If she needs anything."

"It works both ways." Rachel told him. "I have to admit I feel better knowing there's someone in the unit."

Johnno nodded. "We, Quinn's family, we're grateful for everything."

Rachel raised her eyebrows.

"For everything you've done, you're doing for Quinn," he continued. "For letting her rent the unit and for giving her a chance with the job."

"I certainly don't regret that. She's a good worker."

"I know. But believe me, a lot of employers wouldn't, and didn't, consider her. What with her prison record."

Rachel shrugged. "Maybe not. But I've known Quinn a long time. I know she's made mistakes but, well, that was a long time ago."

Johnno gazed down at the dregs of his tea. "I guess we, Becky and Liam and myself, we all felt responsible in part for Quinn and what happened back then. Things were pretty bad at home for her. But the rest of us were married. We had our lives, and I guess we just didn't take the time. If we had, maybe things wouldn't have gone as far as they did."

"You could say the same for the rest of us, her teachers, people who knew her," Rachel said softly. "It was just unfortunate that, well . . ." She left the rest of it unsaid.

They both looked across to where Quinn was helping Katie hang upside down from the climbing frame.

"Anyway," Johnno continued. "I appreciate all you're doing for Quinn. And, come to think of it, for my boy, Kerrod. He loves his job. Always been interested in that sort of thing."

"Well, Kerrod's doing marvelously well, too. Ken tells me he's quick and keen to learn."

They looked up as Quinn joined them, her gaze going from Rachel to her brother as she sat down. "You two look serious."

"We are," said Johnno, winking at Rachel. "I was just telling Rachel how Australia lost by three runs in the last one-day cricket match against the Pakis."

Quinn groaned. "Not boring you with that, too, is he, Rachel? We've heard about nothing else since it happened."

"Now I feel guilty to admit I watched the game myself," laughed Rachel.

"You're a cricket fan?" Quinn asked incredulously.

"Guilty, I'm afraid. I do enjoy the one-day games."

Quinn shook her head. "What about proper sports like tennis or golf?"

Rachel grimaced. "Usually just cricket and rugby league."

"Oh no." Quinn exclaimed in mock horror. "I may have to move right back out of the unit."

"Aren't you staying, Quinn?" Fliss had walked over to join them, and she regarded Quinn with a worried frown.

Quinn stood up and put an arm around the young girl. "I was just teasing your mother about her taste in sports."

Fliss glanced at her mother for confirmation. "Oh. It was a joke. Okay." She grinned. "That's good, because we want you and Katie to stay."

Later that afternoon Rachel and the children were in the pool. Quinn and Katie had gone inside to unpack after Johnno and Nathan left.

"Mind if Katie and I join you?" Quinn asked as she walked across the lawn with the little girl.

"Come on in. You must feel like a cooldown after all that work." Rachel tried not to let her gaze linger on Quinn's body. The white two-piece swimsuit she wore looked great on her, and Rachel felt her heartbeat accelerate as her nerve endings began to tingle.

They splashed in the pool with the children until eventually Quinn and Rachel climbed out and dried off. They sat down on the patio where they could supervise the children.

"I meant to ask you if you could recommend a childcare agency?" Quinn asked. "At the moment Josie's looking after Katie. But it's still a few weeks until Katie starts school, and Josie has a couple of weeks vacation booked from next week, so I don't think it's fair for me to expect her to have Katie on her holiday.

"I've sort of half arranged for Becky's daughter to fill in, but" — Quinn shrugged — "Susie's only sixteen and, although she's sensible enough, I'm a little concerned it's too much responsibility for her."

Rachel explained about the system the local council had of matching up qualified caregivers with children and that all Quinn needed to do was apply.

"It's worked out marvelously well for me with Adam and Fliss. They've been with Cindy for years." Rachel frowned. "As a matter of fact, two of the children Cindy was looking after moved away in the middle of last year. Would you like me to ask Cindy if she's willing to take Katie, too? Cindy's wonderful and very trustworthy. All the council caregivers are screened before they're considered for the scheme."

"That would be great, especially as you recommend her. Not knowing anyone personally has been the thing I've worried about the most. I've been struggling with the idea I have to leave Katie with someone I don't know."

"I'll ring Cindy now and see what she says. If she can't, we'll go through the council channels." Rachel went inside and returned a little later, a frown on her face.

"Well, there's good news and bad news. The good news is, Cindy's happy to take Katie. But the bad news is, she's caught chicken pox," Rachel told Quinn. "She was just going to phone me. Her own kids have just had it, and she thought all would be well for tomorrow. Then this morning she woke up with some spots herself. So we decided it would be best if she didn't have contact with the kids for two weeks."

"What will you do about Adam and Fliss?" Quinn asked.

"I guess I'll have to ask Rose if they can go back up to the farm." Rachel sighed. "I know Rose doesn't mind; she loves having the kids there. But I hate taking advantage of her. If it was only a few days they'd be all right at work, but two weeks is too long." Rachel turned to Quinn. "Will your niece be able to look after Katie, do you think?"

"I guess so."

"What's wrong with Cindy?" asked Fliss. She'd walked up

to them before Rachel realized her daughter was there. "Can't we go to her place tomorrow?"

Rachel explained the situation as Adam and Katie joined them.

"You mean we're going back to the farm?" Adam jumped up and down excitedly. "Great. Can Katie come too? We could show her the animals."

"Oh, I don't know."

"Oh, Mum. It would be fun," Adam began.

"Mummy, can I go up to the farm with Adam and Fliss?" Katie asked. "Adam says there's animals."

"Adam, I haven't even cleared it with your grandmother yet." Rachel turned back to Quinn. "I'm sorry, I didn't mean to —"

"I know." Quinn began toweling Katie dry. "Katie, it's not the right thing to do, inviting yourself somewhere," she began.

"Actually, it was Adam," Fliss told Quinn solemnly. "It wasn't Katie's fault. But Grandma Rose wouldn't mind if Katie came, would she, Mum?"

Rachel shook her head. "I think perhaps I'd better ring your grandmother."

"Do Adam and Fliss have a grandmother, like in my storybooks?" Katie asked her mother, and Quinn shot a quick glance at Rachel before she replied.

"Yes, they do. You did too, but remember I told you your grandmother died when you were just a baby?"

Katie frowned. "Oh yes." She turned to Fliss and Adam. "My grandmother went to heaven."

Adam nodded soberly. "My friend, Josh, at school, his grandmother died too. But we have two grandmothers, so we'll share ours with you if you like."

"You will?" Katie jumped up and down, and Rachel smiled to herself.

"That's very kind of you, Adam," Quinn was saying as Rachel went inside.

Rachel spoke to her mother-in-law, and when she came back she sent the children in to get dressed while she discussed the situation with Quinn.

"You mean your mother-in-law is willing to take on a child she doesn't even know?" Quinn asked incredulously.

Rachel laughed. "Rose adores kids. So does her husband. Over the school holidays they usually have three or four grandchildren there at any given time. But I can understand if you don't want to leave Katie with people you don't know."

"You trust them with Adam and Fliss."

"Yes, I do. As I said, Rose loves kids. It was always a great tragedy for Rose that she couldn't have any more children after she had Rob. Marrying Charlie with his tribe of children and grandchildren has brought Rose such joy."

Quinn bit her lip.

"I'm sorry this has put you in such an awkward position," Rachel said. "I was going to suggest we might drive the kids up to the farm this afternoon. Then you can meet Rose and Charlie, make sure you're satisfied that Katie would be all right. We could stay the night if you like and drive back for work tomorrow. They have a huge old house, so there's plenty of room. What do you think?"

Quinn sighed and looked directly at Rachel. "If you're sure it's okay with Rose? I mean, you did tell her it was me?"

"She knows it's you, Quinn," Rachel said softly. "It makes no difference to Rose."

A few days later Rachel noticed the sporty black BMW Z3 pull into the car park, but it wasn't until she saw the tall blond woman step out of the car and turn to look toward the office that she recognized Laurel Greenwood. R & R Gardening and Landscaping was the last place she would have expected to see the mayor's daughter-in-law. Somehow she couldn't see Laurel repotting plants.

As Rachel watched, Laurel took off her wraparound sunglasses and threw them casually onto the passenger seat. She ran her fingers through her long blond hair, fluffing it away from her face before checking the results in the sideview mirror of her car. Then she straightened her revealing designer T-shirt over her jean-clad hips and walked across to the entrance.

Rachel's eyes narrowed. There was only one reason Rachel could think of why Laurel had turned up here at the Garden Center. She must have come to see Quinn.

Chapter Eleven

As Laurel rounded the building Rachel lost sight of her, so she stood up and walked out of her office. She knew Quinn was over at the Supplies Section helping Old Dave deal with a sudden influx of small trucks and utes, and she could see Phil across the yard in the fernery with a customer. So that left Rachel herself.

Laurel paused, put her hand to her forehead to shield her eyes from the sun, and glanced around the yard. When she noticed Rachel she strode forward.

And as she approached Rachel, Rachel could see that the young woman she'd taught alongside Quinn was the epitome of sophisticated elegance. Her hair was casually tousled, her lipstick unsmudged on her curved lips, and she wore just enough mascara to accentuate her almost violet blue eyes. All in all, Rachel acknowledged, Laurel Greenwood was a very attractive young woman.

When you considered the two friends, Laurel and Quinn, you couldn't imagine that two lives could turn out so differently. Rachel knew that after Quinn had gone to jail Laurel had taken a secretarial course and then secured a job with the City Council. It seemed like no time at all before she started going out with Mike Greenwood, the deputy mayor's son. Within months Mike and Laurel had one of the grandest weddings ever held in the district.

Over the years Rachel had rarely seen Laurel, although she often came across photographs of her in the social pages of the local newspaper. The Greenwoods had moved in different circles to Rachel and Rob, and anyway, they'd been far too busy building their business to socialize all that much.

Looking at this self-possessed young woman, Rachel acknowledged there was barely a trace of the pretty, irresponsible teenager Rachel had taught in school.

Rachel smiled as Laurel approached the desk. "Hello, Laurel. It's been a long time. How are you?"

Laurel's eyebrows rose, and Rachel continued quickly. "I'm Rachel Weston. I was Rachel Richardson. I believe I taught your class some years ago."

"Oh yes," Laurel said detachedly as she glanced around.

"Can I help you with anything?" Rachel asked politely.

Up close, Rachel could see the fine lines around Laurel's eyes and the discontented droop of her mouth. She looked, Rachel decided, a lot older than Quinn, and her skin lacked the healthy glow of Quinn's. Rachel admonished herself testily. It was hardly Laurel's fault she had inherited a fair, delicate complexion while Quinn had the smooth olive skin that tanned so easily.

Laurel seemed to come to a decision, and her pouting

mouth lifted in a forced smile. "Well, yes. I suppose you can help me. You could tell me where to find Quinn Farrelly. I heard she was working here now."

"Yes, you heard correctly," Rachel replied, only just managing to keep the dryness out of her tone. She glanced at her wristwatch. "She's over in the other section, but I'm expecting her back any minute."

The sound of the loader at work had been silent for a couple of minutes, so Quinn was probably on her way back right now.

A small frown of irritation crossed Laurel's face. She also checked the time on the diamond-encrusted watch on her slim wrist. "I guess I can wait then. If you don't think she'll be long."

"She shouldn't be." Rachel knew she could walk over and fetch Quinn, tell her she had a visitor, but with Phil busy with a customer it would leave the office unattended. As there seemed no urgency, Rachel decided Laurel could wait the short time it would take Quinn to walk back to the Garden Center.

"Would you like to sit down? There's a chair in the office."

Laurel glanced in the direction of Rachel's office with barely concealed distaste.

"Or you can look around," Rachel added with some relish. She wasn't sure which would horrify Laurel the most. Sitting in the office or wandering around among the plants.

Laurel's gaze moved over the rows of healthy potted plants, her expression telling Rachel she was totally unmoved by the kaleidoscope of variegated colors. "Oh, I'll just . . . I might look around," she said and, without a backward glance at Rachel, she walked carefully over to the cacti section.

Rachel shrugged and returned to her office. When Phil finished with his customer, no doubt his good looks and charm would be more appealing to Laurel Greenwood.

Unless Colleen's insinuations were true, that Quinn and

Laurel had been more than friends. But Laurel was married and had been for at least ten years. If there was anything in what Colleen intimated, then it would have simply been the experimenting of adolescents. Wouldn't it?

For some reason Rachel didn't care to dwell on that particular question. But she did wonder if Quinn and Laurel had been in touch at all over the years. Quinn certainly hadn't mentioned the young woman who had been her best friend. Yet why would she? Rachel asked herself disdainfully. There was no reason why Quinn should treat Rachel as a confidante.

Rachel touched her keyboard and brought up the accounts she'd been working on before Laurel arrived. It was none of her business, she told herself reproachfully, and she made herself concentrate on her work.

But she was also aware that she was listening for the sound of the opening of the gate between the two sections of the Landscaping Center. The gate squeaked, the hinges needing attention. Rachel and Phil had both been meaning to fix it.

"Well, roll out the red carpet," Phil said sotto voce from the doorway. "Our presence has been graced by her ladyship."

Rachel looked up from her computer.

"The lovely Mrs. Mike Greenwood," he explained with an indication of his head. "I saw you talking to her."

"Oh. Laurel. Yes, she's waiting to see Quinn," Rachel said evenly.

"So she told me before she firmly dismissed me." He looked back into the Garden Center. "Nice packaging, but no center, that one. What does she want with Quinn?"

"Just visiting, I guess. They were friends at school."

"They were? I would have said Quinn was younger," he remarked and paused as he went to walk away. "Rachel?"

Rachel looked up from her screen again.

"Steve told me about Quinn being in jail. I vaguely remember my mother writing to me and telling me about

Mark Herron getting killed, but I just didn't associate that with Quinn. She must . . ." He frowned. "It must be pretty difficult carrying all that around with you."

"Yes, it must," Rachel agreed.

"I guess we all did stupid things when we were young. Most of us didn't get caught or were lucky enough to get away with it without any damage to ourselves or others. What I mean is, Quinn's done her time, and I just wanted to say I'm glad you gave her the job, Rachel. She's great to work with."

Rachel nodded, and Phil walked away.

Only minutes later Rachel heard the squeak of the gate. She shifted in her seat so she could look out the window.

Quinn walked toward the office with her long strides, her short dark hair shining in the sunlight, and something shifted in the region of Rachel's heart. Quinn looked lean and healthy, and the smile she turned on Rachel as she came through the office door made Rachel's mouth go dry. A warm flush of pleasure colored her cheeks.

"Hi, boss." Quinn greeted Rachel. "Old Mr. Sorenson was just in to collect his forest mulch. He's singing Ken's praises over the retaining wall and paving he's just finished. Another satisfied customer."

"That's good to hear. George Sorenson isn't easy to please. Ah, Quinn . . ." Rachel paused. "There's someone to see you."

Quinn raised her eyebrows. "To see me? Who?"

"Laurel Greenwood."

The expression on Quinn's face froze, and Rachel was sure the other woman paled slightly.

"Laurel?" Quinn said softly and then seemed to pull herself together.

"She's out in the Garden Center." Rachel watched Quinn turn to glance out the window. "Have you seen her since . . . since you came home?"

Quinn's gaze returned to Rachel, and she shook her head slightly.

"Do you want to wait here and I'll send her in?" Rachel offered. Quinn frowned.

"No. I'll just . . ." She indicated the door and went to walk away. Then she stopped and turned back to Rachel. "I won't be long."

"Take as long as you like."

Quinn stood silently for long moments before turning and leaving the office.

Before Rachel could prevent herself, she stood up and followed Quinn to the door, watched her pause and glance around, catch sight of Laurel and walk toward her. Rachel guiltily returned to her desk, ashamed of herself. She had no right to spy on Quinn. She made herself concentrate on her accounts, and it was closing time before she caught up on all her paperwork.

Rachel waited while Quinn locked the gates and climbed into the station wagon beside her. She put the car in gear and turned out of the parking lot, following Phil's four-wheel-drive up the road.

They were halfway home before Quinn spoke.

"Laurel was my best friend," she said softly. "Right from first grade."

"Yes, I know."

"You hung out with Janey Watson, didn't you?"

Rachel nodded. "We were friends, too, from the day I started school here after Mum and I came back to town. Janey and her husband live in Mount Isa at the moment. They have four kids, and Janey and I still keep in touch."

"Laurel and I were . . . pretty tight."

Rachel sat silently, waiting for Quinn to continue, and she realized her hands were gripping the steering wheel. She made herself relax a little, knowing she was half-afraid of any confidence Quinn might want to share.

"You know, the only thing I remember from that night was, well, afterward." Quinn shifted in her seat, adjusted her seat belt. "Looking for Laurel." She ran her hands absently along her thighs, let her hands rest on her knees, her long, thin fingers in Rachel's peripheral vision.

"I still have nightmares about it. Of the absolute darkness. The silence. The smell of petrol and beer and blood. And desperately looking for Laurel."

Rachel slowed the car and took the road leading up to the estate, past a clump of leafy gum trees that overlooked the river. At the height of summer the river was barely a creek, shallow potholes of water strung among the rocks and sandy silt that made up the watercourse. Not far from here the creek branched off the river, the same creek that flowed close by the road where Quinn's accident had happened. Rachel headed the car up the hill.

"Becky wrote and told me when Laurel got married." Quinn sighed. "Laurel said they had a big house up on the hill behind town. And that sports car she was driving, Mike gave it to her for her birthday."

Rachel felt her lips twist.

"Seems she's done well for herself," said Quinn, her tone completely inscrutable.

"Yes, I suppose she has," Rachel agreed inadequately.

"I could never picture Laurel marrying Mike Greenwood. I mean, she couldn't stand him."

Rachel felt Quinn looking at her and she glanced sideways, her gaze momentarily meeting Quinn's.

"Life's funny, isn't it? You always seemed to fob off Rob Weston, and then you married him. And back then when Mike started showing an interest in Laurel, she said he was a stuck-up rich kid, told him to take a hike. Then she married him."

Rachel shifted uneasily in her seat. Yes, she'd married Rob, but she'd hazard a guess that Laurel hadn't married Mike for the same reason that Rachel had married Rob. Or had she? Did she have more in common with Laurel than anyone knew?

Turning the car into the driveway, Rachel used the remote to open the garage door.

"They, Laurel and Mike, have three boys." Quinn gave a soft laugh as Rachel stopped the car inside the garage and turned off the engine. "I also can't imagine Laurel with kids. Never in a million years would I have seen her as a mother figure. But then again, no doubt she felt the same about me having Katie. She said as much."

They both climbed out of the car, Quinn following Rachel into the house as the garage door slid down behind them. Quinn walked over to the door between the house and the unit.

"Quinn." Rachel said quickly. "I . . . Want to share a salad?"

Quinn looked back at Rachel, her hand on the doorknob. "I can't tonight." Her eyes didn't meet Rachel's. "But thanks, Rachel. I'm going out tonight."

"Oh. That's okay then. I'll see you tomorrow."

Quinn gave a nod. "Love changes everything, doesn't it?" she said cryptically as she disappeared into her unit.

Quinn and Rachel were in the pool after what had turned out to be a very long day for both of them. Quinn had driven up to the farm to see Katie, stayed the night, and driven back in time to start work this morning. And Rachel had slept badly, alone in the house, refusing to acknowledge the thought that she had missed Quinn's presence in the adjoining unit.

Apart from that, she couldn't seem to prevent herself from thinking about Quinn and Laurel, seeing them as carefree teenagers, as the adults they were today. And she wondered for the hundredth time where Quinn had gone that night after Laurel appeared at the Garden Center.

Had Quinn arranged to meet Laurel? Rachel was disgusted with herself for the direction of her thoughts, yet she couldn't seem to reign in her fertile imagination. And she'd had to drag herself out of bed to go to work this morning.

On top of that they'd been so busy at the Garden Center today they'd all barely had time for more than a hurried snack on the run at lunchtime.

As the day passed, clouds formed and the humidity rose, making everyone hot, sticky, and irritable. So when Quinn had suggested stopping at a local casual restaurant for dinner when they finally left the Garden Center, Rachel couldn't get into the air-conditioned restaurant quick enough.

By the time they arrived home, by mutual consent, they both headed outside for a swim.

Quinn leaned back against the side of the pool and ran her fingers through her wet hair.

Chapter Twelve

"This is the coolest I've been all day. What a scorcher." She looked across at Rachel. "I had a good time up at the farm again yesterday, and the car's running much better since Charlie had a look at it. Your mother-in-law and her husband are very nice people."

"I knew you'd like Rose and Charlie. They're two of the kindest people I know," Rachel agreed, submerging herself to her chin in the cool, silky water. "And I'm glad you feel confident enough to leave Katie up there with them."

"When Rose let Katie hold one of those little yellow chicks last weekend I knew I was lost," Quinn said wryly.

"I noticed."

"It's difficult to, you know, I just want Katie to have

a . . ." Quinn shook her head. "If I say I just want Katie to have a better life than I had, it sounds as though I had a miserable, deprived childhood. But I didn't, really." She slid a glance at Rachel. "Not like Johnno and Liam and Becky did."

Rachel didn't know what to say.

"Everyone said my father had mellowed a bit by the time I arrived," Quinn continued. "But he'd still knock Johnno or Liam across the room if they looked sideways at him. Liam became an expert at making himself scarce, but my father was always hardest on Johnno."

"Did he ever hit you?" Rachel asked quietly.

Quinn shrugged. "Occasionally. Not like he took to the boys and Becky, though." She gave a mirthless laugh. "Now that's something for the psychologists. He physically abused the other three but usually left me alone. They turned out to be model citizens, while I'm the only bad apple in the Farrelly barrel."

"You were never that," Rachel said quickly. "Just, well, high-spirited."

Quinn laughed. "There are a lot of people who would say you were being too kind, Rachel. I'm afraid I was a lost cause back then."

Rachel knew this had been the general consensus.

"But I distinctly remember the last time my father hit my mother. I mean, he still got drunk and abusive, but I never saw him hit her again." Quinn went on. "I guess I must have been four or five because Johnno would have been Kerrod's age.

"Dad had been drinking all afternoon, and Becky and my mother were cooking dinner. Looking back, I can see that when my father started to drink the whole house seemed to take on a gathering pressure. It was sort of poised, waiting for the explosion. My mother looked drawn and pinched. We kids kept as out of the way as we could.

"Anyway, that particular evening I hid under the kitchen

table when I heard Dad coming. He abused my mother about what she'd cooked, and food and crockery went flying.

"Then he slapped my mother and she fell backward onto the stove, seared her arm on the burner. My mother and Becky were crying; my father was swearing. And then Johnno came home. When he saw what was happening, he went berserk. He'd never retaliated until that night. He yelled at Dad that he was a drunkard and a coward. Fists started flying, and my mother was screaming.

"The neighbors must have called the police, as they usually had to do, but by the time they arrived my father was out cold and Johnno had a broken hand from hitting him.

"I remember looking at my father lying there in the mess on the kitchen floor and thinking he was dead. I thought they'd take Johnno away and we'd never be safe. That's when I added to the pandemonium by getting hysterical. It took two cops to pry my arms from around Johnno's leg." Quinn grimaced. "Just another day with your typical dysfunctional family."

"I'm sorry, Quinn," Rachel said, feeling inadequate. "It must have been awful for you."

Quinn shook her head. "You know, when I was young I used to be so angry all the time, mostly with my mother. Which was unreasonable. But I could never figure out why she stayed with him, or why she didn't at least fight back. In retrospect, I think my mother had given up long before I was born. Maybe she stayed in the beginning because she cared, but in the end she didn't leave because she didn't care."

They were silent for long seconds.

"But I was devastated when I couldn't get home for my mother's funeral." A long sigh escaped from Quinn's lips. "I'd had a couple of scares during my pregnancy when they thought I might miscarry. When Becky rang me and told me Mum had died I was in hospital, due to have Katie by caesarian the day of the funeral.

93

"I wanted to drive home, but Becky told me in no uncertain terms to do no such thing. The decision was taken out of my hands because I went into labor that night and Katie was born the next morning. So there was no way I could make it to the funeral."

Her gaze met Rachel's. "When I got pregnant with Katie I swore I'd never put either of us in the sort of situation I'd been in as a child."

"Was that . . .?" Rachel swallowed. "Was that why you left Katie's father?"

Rachel couldn't see Quinn's expression in the almost darkness, but she felt an invisible barrier come down between them.

"No," Quinn said at last. "No, that wasn't the reason." She glanced at Rachel and away again. "I guess we just didn't love each other enough."

Rachel wanted to ask more, but at that moment a flash of lightning lit the tumble of clouds across the sky.

"Oh! Ho! Looks like the promised storm has arrived." Quinn turned and put the palms of her hands on the edge of the pool, effortlessly springing out of the water.

Thunder growled around them, and Rachel moved over to the steps to find Quinn there before her. Quinn leaned down and offered Rachel her hand. Rachel took it and, with a tug, Quinn propelled her up and out onto the side of the pool.

Suddenly Rachel realized they were barely a foot apart, and she instinctively went to step backward. Quinn reached out, took hold of Rachel again, steadying her so she didn't overbalance backward into the water.

Quinn's hands rested on the curve of Rachel's hips, and now Rachel's body was mere inches from Quinn's. They stood immobile, the space between them alive, as charged as the air surging about the burgeoning clouds above them.

Rachel's entire body tensed, waiting for Quinn to move toward her, wanting her to so badly.

Another bright flash lit the sky as the first large drops of rain splashed down on their damp bodies.

"We'll get wet," Rachel said inanely.

"Yes," Quinn replied, her voice low and throaty, and her hands set Rachel free.

They made a dash for the shelter of the patio roof as the rain came teeming down.

"Not that we could get much wetter," Quinn shouted above the noise of the rain beating down upon the unlined roof.

Rachel made a pretence of laughing. Her entire body burned, tension holding her stiffly. Her nerve endings drummed in tune with the rain as she yearned for Quinn's touch, the feel of Quinn's body against her own. If only she had the courage to . . .

"We'd better go inside," Quinn said at last. "See you in the morning."

Rachel nodded, unable to trust her voice. And then Quinn was ducking under the carport and disappearing through the back door of the unit, leaving Rachel on her own with her tortured thoughts.

Turning unsteadily, Rachel went inside. She stood in the laundry and automatically peeled off her wet swimsuit. When she was naked she began to towel herself dry.

She rubbed the soft towel over her breasts and her nipples hardened again, the ache of arousal inside her a physical pain. Why was she such a coward? Why didn't she just . . .?

And suddenly she found herself crying, long sobs racking her body. She put the towel to her face and wept.

"I don't seem to be able to get used to the quietness of the house when the kids are up at the farm," Rachel said as they walked through from the garage after work the next day.

When they were rostered to work together, they usually traveled together in Rachel's station wagon.

Rachel still felt strung out from the emotional overload the evening before, and the storm had had little to do with it. Now it seemed safer somehow, talking about the children.

"I feel sort of unfinished myself, with Katie not here. I haven't really spent any time apart from her since she was born."

"She'll be fine up there. Rose is one of the most sensible people I know," Rachel reassured her again as they walked into the living room.

"I know. I'm not really concerned about that. And I also know I can't keep her in cotton batting. She'll be starting school soon, and I've always known that would be a wrench. I mean, Katie's been to preschool, so I don't know why the fact that she's going to school bothers me."

"I think it's because going to school is their sort of symbolic first big step away from you. At least, that's how I saw it with Fliss and Adam."

"You're probably right." Quinn sighed. "I guess I have to learn to let go some time, so I might as well start getting used to it now."

"I think most mothers feel the same. I know I felt absolutely devastated when I had to leave both of mine at school on their first days. Fliss and Adam both went off happily to play with the other kids while I bawled all the way home. Both times." Rachel smiled and shook her head. "Rob told me I should have been happy they were both outgoing and well-adjusted."

"They are that. They're both great kids."

"The three of them are."

"So I guess we must have done something right, then." Quinn glanced at her wristwatch. "Almost dinner time. How about I order us a pizza?"

"Pizza would be great," Rachel was more than a little pleased that Quinn wanted to spend more time with her, and she studiously ignored the small spurt of concern inside her that implied being alone with Quinn wasn't such a good idea. "But we can go dutch treat."

"No. I'm buying." Quinn walked over to the phone. "What's your preferred topping?"

With the pizza ordered, Rachel decided to make them each a small salad. They moved about the kitchen preparing it, Quinn talking about a couple of demanding customers she'd had that day, making Rachel laugh delightedly at her true-to-life impersonations.

"Want to watch a movie while we eat?" Rachel asked as they returned to the living room. "I've got a small collection of tapes."

"Sure. What have you got to offer?" Quinn walked over to the video cabinet.

Rachel made an issue of settling on the couch, glad Quinn had her back to her and couldn't see Rachel's flushed face. To offer? Rachel wished she could tell Quinn what she'd really like.

"The top shelf are mine, and on the bottom shelf are the kids' movies," she said quickly, and Quinn went down on her haunches to read the titles.

"*Sleeping Beauty. Care Bears.*" She turned and grinned at Rachel. "Let's be devils, seeing as we're alone. Let's have one from the top shelf."

Rachel laughed. "There's nothing too avant-garde, I'm afraid. You choose."

Quinn pulled out a video. "*The Full Monty.* Great. I missed this one. But I guess you've seen it." She turned to Rachel.

"That's okay. It was ages ago. I could see it again."

"It's supposed to be funny."

"It is. But there's an underlying sadness. It's good, though, because the characters are wonderful and they're making a positive out of a negative situation. I think you'll enjoy it." Rachel set her salad down on the coffee table and stood up. "I forgot drinks."

Quinn followed Rachel into the kitchen, and Rachel opened the fridge door. "I've got Coke or lemonade, fruit juice, and there's a couple of beers, too. What do you feel like?"

Rachel paused, waiting for Quinn's reply. She straightened, a cold can of beer in her hand, and she looked around, her gaze meeting Quinn's.

Quinn was leaning against the doorjamb, her face pale, a closed expression on her face as she glanced at the can of beer in Rachel's hand. "Coke will be fine," she said evenly.

Rachel swallowed. "I'm sorry, I . . ." She slid the beer back into the fridge. "Coke it is," she said quickly and handed the drink to Quinn. She took a fruit juice for herself. When she turned back to Quinn, the other woman was looking at the drink in her hand.

"I haven't had a beer since the night it happened," Quinn said quietly. "I can't even bear the smell of it."

Rachel put her hand on Quinn's arm. "That's understandable, Quinn. I'm sorry. I didn't even think —"

"It wasn't your fault. I just, it's strange, really. I don't seem to have a problem with driving or being driven, but the smell of beer seems to bring it all back."

Rachel's hand rubbed the smooth skin of Quinn's arm. Quinn looked down at the point of contact and then back at Rachel. As their eyes met, something shifted in Rachel's chest. Suddenly that same heavy tension seemed to envelop them, hold them captive.

Rachel could feel herself being drawn into the clear gray depths of Quinn's eyes, her senses swirling, her control slipping. She couldn't seem to catch her breath. Her gaze fell, her eyes settling on the full curve of Quinn's lips, and all she wanted was to touch them with her own, taste them.

Chapter Thirteen

Rachel suspected she was moving forward when the buzzing of the doorbell cut between them like a knife.

They both jumped, and Rachel clutched at her fruit juice as it slipped from her hand. She caught it before it hit the floor.

"That'll be the pizza," Quinn said softly, and she was the first to move toward the door.

As they ate their meal they watched the movie Quinn had chosen, although Rachel found it difficult to concentrate on the plot. All she could hear was the thunderous beating of her heart as it pounded inside her. And her focus seemed set on the tanned length of Quinn's bare legs so close beside her on the couch.

That moment in the kitchen when she had been so aware of Quinn had left her shaken and restless. All the more so because she suspected Quinn had felt the tension too. This fascination she felt for Quinn was growing steadily, and it frightened her as much as it had all those years ago. Probably more so, she told herself.

Back then the attraction was all mixed up with a hundred other fears. Fear about *why* she was attracted to Quinn. Fear of Quinn's reaction if she so much as suspected that Rachel felt the way she did. Fear that her mother and her family and her friends would find out. Fear of her disturbing secret, the alienness of knowing she felt this way about another woman. It had burned inside her, terrifying her.

Now she was older, could allow the word *lesbian* to formulate in her mind. Not that that removed all the old fears, but maturity had given her the skills to put most of those fears into perspective.

If she'd possessed those same skills twelve years ago, would it have made any difference to her choices? Rachel asked herself. She thought about her children. Although she had never considered herself to be overly maternal, she knew she couldn't imagine her life without them.

And Rob? Her husband. What about him? Her mind threw up scenes from the past, of tall, teenaged Rob, his long unruly hair tied back in a ponytail, teasing her in front of his mates.

At some stage during their teenage years, Rob's teasing had ceased and he'd simply followed her around, wanting her to go out with him. Rachel had been polite but aloof. Sandy and Colleen had insisted Rob had had a crush on her, and Rachel had denied it, filled with embarrassment.

When Rachel realized how she felt about Quinn she'd been so perturbed by her feelings she'd surprised both herself and Rob by agreeing to his invitation to the movies. To go out with a young man was the accepted thing to do, and Rachel had been so anxious about her feelings for Quinn she'd decided dating Rob was the only thing she could do to put her tottering world right. The alternative was totally beyond her consideration.

And Rachel couldn't deny that she'd enjoyed the social conventions of going out with Rob. Her mother was pleased, and so was Rob's. It was what young women did. No other scenario was acceptable.

Rachel pushed the past out of her mind and made herself concentrate on the movie Quinn had chosen. When the scene came where the two men kissed, Rachel felt her stomach clench and her face grow hot. Could Quinn hear the thundering beat of her heart? Surely she must. But Quinn refrained from commenting.

"That was good," she said when the movie eventually finished and Rachel rewound the tape. "Feel like watching anything else?"

Rachel shrugged. "I don't mind." She glanced at her wristwatch. "I guess we may as well, seeing as we're both off tomorrow. I'll take all this away while you look for something else to watch." She began clearing away the remains of their meal as Quinn looked through the movies again. When she came back into the room Quinn had flipped the channels and found a James Bond movie.

"How about some mindless adventure with the indestructible 007?"

Rachel laughed. "Only if it's a Sean Connery one."

"You're in luck."

They talked occasionally as they half watched the movie until Rachel realized that Quinn was yawning. Regretfully she turned to suggest they call it a night when she realized Quinn's eyelids had dropped to her cheeks and she was breathing evenly, obviously asleep.

Rachel watched her surreptitiously. The dark slashes of her eyelashes on her cheeks. Her mouth, relaxed and inviting. The curve of her jaw line. Her long neck. Rachel let her gaze linger on the rise and fall of Quinn's chest, the swell of her breasts, and she knew with absolute and futile certainty that she had fallen in love with Quinn Farrelly.

And this, she knew, was no adolescent crush. There was no way she would be able to push these feelings to the back of her mind. What she felt for Quinn was all consuming.

Now that she had admitted it to herself, she realized she'd known all along that Quinn was special. She was barely surprised and felt almost lightheaded. But with the wonder of it came an almost unbearable sadness.

Where could such an inappropriate love lead her? Nowhere! she told herself painfully. It was no more acceptable now than it had been over a dozen years ago.

Tears welled behind Rachel's eyes, but she dashed them away. One thing was certain. She surely wasn't going to follow the same path she had last time.

Her attraction to Quinn all those years ago had sent her panic-stricken and terrified into Rob Weston's waiting arms. This time she saw she had two choices. She'd have to learn to live with this, try to bury it deeply inside her, the way she had all those years ago. Or she could take a chance on making the biggest mistake of her life and confess to Quinn how she felt.

Rachel knew she couldn't do that. She didn't want to chance losing Quinn's friendship.

But what if she did chance it? Rachel couldn't even guess at Quinn's reaction. Would she find Rachel's attraction repulsive?

Rachel thought about Colleen's revelations. What if . . .? It was only hearsay, Rachel reminded herself, and her heart sank. She knew she couldn't act on the off chance that a snippet of twelve-year-old gossip held any truth.

Switching off the television, Rachel moved gently, standing up slowly so that she didn't wake Quinn. It was too warm for Quinn to get cold, so Rachel decided to leave her there. A cushion supported her head, so she looked reasonably comfortable. When Quinn eventually woke up, she could slip through the door into her unit or stretch out properly on the couch.

Rachel climbed the stairs and went straight into the *en suite*. She took a shower and pulled on the light oversize sleeveless tank top she wore as a nightshirt.

Stretching out on the bed, she tried to relax her tensed body. She felt . . . Rachel examined her feelings, skirting the truth. She felt *aroused, turned on*. Whatever the current term was these days. She swallowed as her body grew hotter.

She couldn't remember the last time she'd felt quite like this. She wondered if she ever had.

Then she was thinking about Rob, how it had been between them. A wave of guilt clutched at her as she thought about her late husband. Had she shortchanged Rob? He'd been a good husband, had never demanded more of her than she'd been willing to give. And when it came to the physical side of their marriage, Rachel hadn't exactly been all that enthusiastic.

Rachel couldn't say she'd disliked sex with Rob. It had simply never been earth shattering for her. She realized she could have lived without it. Had Rob known that? With a sigh Rachel acknowledged he probably had. Yet with his usual good humor, Rob had let her set the pace.

They'd been dating for months before they'd made love, and it had happened then simply because Rachel felt it was expected of her. They had parked down by the riverbank, found a spot away from the other parked cars, and Rob had suggested they get into the back of his old car. It would be more comfortable, he'd said.

How anyone could find any comfort scrabbling around in the back of a car, Rachel couldn't imagine. They were both inexperienced and floundered around, trying to find the right contact. Rachel had grown tense and unsure. Rob admitted later that he had been the same. It was over almost before it began and, the discomfort aside, it had been a non-event as far as Rachel was concerned.

Although they'd grown a little more proficient during their engagement, Rachel had always known as a lover she would never set the world on fire. She felt herself flush. Apart from those rare moments when she'd let her guard down, allowed herself to think about Quinn Farrelly, about kissing her, making love to her. And Quinn was just downstairs.

Rachel sat up, her heart pounding away inside her. She wiped her hand over her eyes and gulped a breath. This situation was getting way out of hand. When Quinn had moved in, Rachel had suspected she'd be on shaky ground. Now she knew she was.

Rearranging her pillows, Rachel tried to get comfortable in her suddenly lonely bed. She tossed for what seemed like hours, brief snatches of memories returning to taunt her. And all of them featured Quinn Farrelly.

Eventually Rachel sat up again and flicked on the bedside lamp. Maybe she'd read for a while. Then she remembered she'd left her book in the living room. Unreasonably, she cursed her lack of foresight.

There was no way she could sleep at the moment. And thinking about Quinn wasn't helping her insomnia. She'd have to go downstairs, make herself a cup of tea, and find her book.

She slipped from the bed and padded barefoot along the passage and down the stairs. Moonlight poured in through the glass feature wall in front of the stairway. Maybe Quinn had woken, gone through to her own bed. No such luck, of course.

Tiptoeing across the living room, Rachel quietly skirted the couch and carefully picked up her novel from the coffee table. She turned to go into the kitchen, but she froze as Quinn murmured. Turning around, Rachel moved silently back toward the couch and gazed down at Quinn.

Quinn was still asleep, but now she was stretched out fully on the couch. The light from the full moon bathed the side of her face in muted shades, yet Rachel could see the dark smudge of her lashes resting on her cheek and the relaxed curve of her mouth.

Sudden guilt clutched at Rachel and she moved away, continuing into the kitchen. She had no right to watch Quinn like that when Quinn was unaware of her covert regard. It was tantamount to spying.

Quietly Rachel pushed the kitchen door to and flicked on the subdued light on the range hood over the stove. She filled the kettle and plugged it in, taking down a mug and the teabags.

Rachel was waiting for the kettle to boil when she heard a noise from the living room. She stiffened. There it was again.

She crossed to the door and gently pulled it open. The murmurings became a whimper and, concerned now, Rachel crossed to the couch. Was Quinn ill? Rachel leaned over and then realized Quinn was still asleep, that she was dreaming.

As Rachel watched, Quinn began to move her head agitatedly, her hands clutching at the couch, murmurs of despair breaking from her.

"No! No!" Quinn cried, obviously distressed. "No! Petrol. Have to . . . Laurel. Laurel. Please. Must . . . No! No!"

Rachel reached out and lightly put her hand on Quinn's shoulder. Quinn sat up immediately, gasping for breath. Rachel came around the edge of the couch and sank down beside her, wrapped her arms around the other woman.

"Quinn. It's okay. You're awake now. It was just a dream."

Quinn continued to gulp deep steadying breaths, and Rachel crooned soothingly to her.

"It's me. Rachel. You're all right now. You were dreaming."

Quinn stiffened suddenly, clutching at Rachel, her hands biting into the flesh of Rachel's arm.

"It's okay." Rachel continued to soothe her quietly, as she would have done if Quinn had been Fliss or Adam and they'd woken in fright.

Eventually Quinn's breathing slowed. She took one long, deep breath. "I'm sorry." Her fingers relaxed their panic-stricken grip on Rachel's arm.

Rachel's pulses raced as she felt the warmth of Quinn's breath on her cheek. She moved slightly so she could look at Quinn. "Was it the same dream? The one you told me about?" she asked softly, and Quinn nodded.

"I always seem to wake up when . . . I mean, it always leaves me with the impression I'm about to get to the end of the terror, but just when I'm about to I get so, well, agitated, I wake up. I never . . . It never ends," she finished flatly.

"It must be terrifying," Rachel said, and she pulled Quinn back into the circle of her arms. Then she realized she was absently rubbing Quinn's back, and she stopped, let her hand fall away.

Quinn straightened, and their eyes met. Neither of them broke that intimate contact, and suddenly the timbre of the moment changed radically.

Rachel's mouth went dry, and she felt a renewal of tension rising inside her. She was filled with a growing elation, followed just as suddenly by that age-old fear. She couldn't allow herself to be this close to Quinn. It was the height of foolishness.

But if she leaned just slightly forward, her traitorous senses encouraged her, her lips would find Quinn's. She could . . . Rachel moved abruptly, pushing herself to her feet.

Quinn looked up at her, her gray eyes dark, glowing pools in the semidarkness.

Rachel's gaze focused on Quinn's mouth, the curving fullness of her lips, and as she watched she was sure the tip of Quinn's tongue came out to dampen them. Rachel's knees went weak with wanting.

"I, we . . . I mean, I have to . . ." She drew a steadying breath. "The kettle's boiling."

She started to walk back toward the kitchen, but she stopped, looked back at Quinn. "I was making tea."

The kettle's whistle became shriller, and after one last look at Quinn, Rachel hurried into the kitchen. She reached out, fumbled for the switch, turned off the kettle. Silence engulfed her, and she stood unmoving, not turning around, knowing instinctively that Quinn had followed her into the kitchen. She felt the other woman's presence as though Quinn had reached out and touched her, run her fingers down Rachel's spine. Rachel shivered.

"Would you like a cup?" she asked, moving toward the counter to disguise her involuntary movement.

"Yes. Please."

Quinn's voice sounded a little unsteady, but Rachel told herself that Quinn had just woken from a nightmare. She would be upset.

Rachel moved around, setting out another mug, the sugar bowl. Eventually she allowed herself the luxury of a glance in Quinn's direction.

Quinn was just inside the kitchen and stood with one hip propped against a countertop, her arms wrapped around herself as though she was cold. And her eyes continued to follow Rachel's movements.

"Sugar. No milk," Rachel said inanely as she went through the tea making ritual, her hands far from steady.

"Did I . . . Did I say anything?" Quinn asked, and Rachel turned to look at her. "When I was dreaming," she elaborated.

Rachel shook her head. "No. I don't think so. At least, nothing coherent. It sounded as though you were in pain. At first I thought you were ill."

Quinn nodded.

"Does it happen often?"

Quinn sighed. "Often enough."

"It must be dreadful to have to relive it all the time," Rachel said softly.

Quinn walked across the kitchen, resting her weight on her hands on the sink as she gazed out the back window into the garden. With the range hood light on and the yard in darkness, Rachel knew Quinn wouldn't be able to see a thing out there.

"It's as though I'm watching it all happen to someone else. I see the car. The road. The headlights cutting through the blackness. I feel the speed. Then, at the corner, the car rolls. Over and over. In slow motion. The noise is almost unbearable. The doors fly open and it rolls again. There's this grinding, crunching, sickening thud. And then the silence.

"I see myself crawling through the darkness. I can make out the vague shape of the car. It's upside down, and the front seems to be buried in the creek bank. I can't see the others.

"My mouth sort of fills with sand or water or something, and I can't breathe, and I start to fight my way out of whatever's holding me back." Quinn drew a shaky breath. "I think that's when I wake up."

Rachel took a few steps toward Quinn and then stopped when she started speaking again.

"They told me I was thrown out of the car and into the water. Luckily it wasn't too deep and there were no rocks or branches where I landed. Laurel wasn't so lucky. She was thrown clear too, but they think she broke her leg on a submerged tree or something in the water. Mark died in the car, and Graham was thrown out and the car rolled on him. That's how he lost his leg."

Quinn's back tensed, and Rachel reached out, put a comforting hand on Quinn's shoulder, her fingers registering the warmth of her skin beneath her shirt.

"I must have passed out after I crawled from the creek. I don't remember any of that or how I got to the hospital. They told me all this later." Her shoulders tensed even more.

"I shouldn't have been driving. I was . . ." Quinn turned around to look at Rachel, her gray eyes reflecting her pain. Her lips twisted derisively. "What was it we used to call it? *Legless?* I was totally legless." She frowned. "I can't imagine driving when I . . . I never had before."

Quinn rubbed a hand over her eyes. "I'd been guilty of a

lot of things but I'd never driven before when I'd been drinking. I'd never been so out of control that I . . ." She shook her head, and her tensed muscles slumped. Her eyes met Rachel's. "I guess it only took that one time," she said flatly.

"The four of you had been drinking, Quinn. Not just you," Rachel reminded her, and Quinn's gaze dropped, her dark lashes shielding her expression.

"I've never found much consolation in that."

Rachel swallowed, not knowing quite what to say. "Maybe not, but it is true. Some of the responsibility had to fall on the other three surely."

Quinn looked back at Rachel. "Well. It's all in the past. And not even my nightmares will change it."

Rachel yearned to take Quinn in her arms. Her hand that still rested on Quinn's shoulder slipped downward until her fingers gently rested around Quinn's forearm. Her eyes met Quinn's, and suddenly Rachel knew the tension, that dangerous, exhilarating tension, was back.

Rachel's own muscles reacted, and she knew by the sudden stillness of Quinn's body that the other woman felt it too. Rachel tensed as a mixture of anticipation and apprehension enveloped her. It was a heavy weight. In the air around them. On her skin. In the buzzing inside her head.

She watched as Quinn's gaze shifted to focus on the place where Rachel's hand rested on the smooth skin of her arm. Guiltily Rachel let her hand fall to her side, her fingers nervously fidgeting with the material in her nightshirt.

"I . . . The tea . . . I should make the tea." But Rachel's feet refused to move. She couldn't seem to get her keyed-up muscles to take direction. She stood there, one step away from Quinn, wanting to reach out to her, touch her, pull her into her arms, hold her close. She wanted to hold Quinn more than she'd wanted anything in her life.

They both stood there, unmoving, and Rachel felt an incendiary heat wash over her. Any moment she would ignite.

She watched the shadow of a pulse beating erratically at the base of Quinn's throat, and she knew her own thundered in unison. Her gaze rose to Quinn's mouth, saw the slight tremor of her lips, knew Quinn's breathing was as shallow as her own. And eventually she looked into Quinn's eyes.

Rachel felt like she was drowning in them, in their clear gray depths. She was being drawn into a midnight sea, into the swirling vortex. She could almost feel the oily smoothness of the ocean, washing her skin, drawing her downward, surrounding her.

"I desperately want to kiss you."

Chapter Fourteen

Rachel saw Quinn's lips move, heard exactly what Quinn had said in her so familiar voice, yet her brain refused to compute the meaning of those impassioned words.

I desperately want to kiss you.

The silence that fell became impossibly heavier. Rachel's whole body seemed to sing with a tension that was almost painful. She wanted to move. She wanted to speak. Yet she seemed unable to reply or respond.

And I desperately want to kiss you too.

But the words wouldn't come.

"I'm sorry, Rachel," Quinn said softly, her eyes not meeting Rachel's. Then she moved, walked slowly around Rachel and back out toward the living room.

For long moments Rachel just stood there, Quinn's husky apology ringing in her ears. Then she was dragging ragged breaths into her lungs, and she hurried after Quinn.

She was standing by the couch, running her hand through her short hair, her back to Rachel.

"Quinn . . ." Rachel swallowed as her voice broke.

Quinn turned back to her, held up her hand. "It's all right, Rachel. I shouldn't have said anything. I knew it would freak you out."

"What makes you think that?" Rachel asked, knowing it was a plausible question. She hadn't given Quinn any reason to think otherwise. Why wouldn't Quinn think it would upset her when she'd built this so very proper facade around herself? When she'd stood there in the kitchen like a traumatized Victorian maiden needing a whiff of burned feather?

Quinn shook her head, ran her hand over her eyes. "Just forget I said it. Please."

"It probably should freak me out," Rachel continued as evenly as she could, and she saw a small frown cross Quinn's brow. "But it doesn't."

Quinn's head jerked up, her eyes locking with Rachel's. "Rachel, do you know what you're . . .?"

"I know I don't want you to walk away." Rachel swallowed again, took a small step forward, reached out, and touched a shaking hand to Quinn's cheek.

"God, Rachel," Quinn said brokenly. She moved her head until her lips were caressing the palm of Rachel's hand.

They stood like that for long moments, and then Quinn's arms reached out, slid around Rachel, and drew her close.

Rachel melted into her, felt the glorious softness of her lips on Quinn's at last, after years of secret, feverish imagining. She tasted the sweetness of Quinn's tongue, and she was aflame with the heady excitement of her touch.

Part of her registered that she could feel every curve, every nuance of Quinn's body. Her hipbones pressed against

Rachel's, her flat stomach, the swell of her small breasts, and she hoped desperately that her own body felt as good to Quinn.

Quinn rested her hips against the back of the couch and pulled Rachel closer still. Her lips nibbled Rachel's sensitive earlobe, followed the line of her jaw, almost reached her mouth. Paused.

Quinn's lips slid slowly upward, over Rachel's flushed cheek, to tenderly kiss each eyelid, the tip of her nose and then, eons later, to find Rachel's mouth again. Her lips caressed Rachel's, her tongue teased and then slipped inside.

And Rachel moaned. She'd never been kissed quite like this before. Quinn's kiss seemed to spread down into her core, her very soul. She felt as though Quinn had reached inside her, encircled her heart, held it cocooned, cradled safely in her strong hands. Rachel's whole body tuned to the other woman.

So this was what it felt like to kiss Quinn Farrelly, a small part of her reflected as her nerve endings danced like marionettes gone mad. All those years ago, Rachel had wondered. And when she'd dropped her guard during the ensuing years she'd done more fantasizing about how soft Quinn's lips would be, how it would feel to hold her close.

Now Rachel knew.

The feel of Quinn's lips on her own was more, so very much more exciting, more electrifying, than she had ever imagined it could be.

How she wished she hadn't wasted all those years. She wanted Quinn to go on kissing her forever.

Quinn's hands played over Rachel's back, down the length of her spine, and it seemed to Rachel that Quinn's deft fingers sought out every indentation, traced every vertebra, made them her own. Then her hands slid downward to cup Rachel's buttocks, pressing Rachel impossibly closer to her warm, long body.

One of Quinn's legs insinuated itself between Rachel's legs, her bare skin smooth and vibrant. Quinn's thigh pressed between Rachel's thighs, and Rachel groaned softly as arrows of unadulterated desire centered between her legs. Spirals of wanting clutched at her, made her catch her breath. Her muscles went weak, and she sagged against Quinn.

Quinn's lips surrendered Rachel's to slide down the curve of her throat, pushing aside the strap of her tank top, continuing over Rachel's smooth shoulder. And Rachel's body sang where Quinn touched her. Quinn's mouth returned to tease Rachel's lips, then moved downward again, following the low neckline of her nightshirt, over the swell of Rachel's left breast, her right breast, back to settle tantalizingly at the top of the thrilling valley between them.

Rachel tensed again. Every nerve ending in her body was alive, waiting, totally tuned to Quinn's so arousing touch.

Then Quinn drew back, leaving Rachel's skin cold where her warm lips had rested. She looked into Rachel's eyes.

Please. Don't stop. Rachel entire body seemed to scream the entreaty into the silence.

"Rachel?" Quinn said softly, her voice low and thick, seducing Rachel even more. "I want to . . ." She drew a shallow breath. "I want to make love to you."

Rachel's senses soared. She knew she was so aroused she'd fall through space any second. She managed a small smile. "You mean there's more?" she asked, her voice raw and broken.

"If you want more," Quinn said. Her gaze never wavered from Rachel's, her gray eyes almost black in the dim light, the curve of her wonderful lips promising so much.

Rachel let her hands move lightly over the swell of Quinn's hips, pause at her waist, her fingers splayed out over Quinn's flat midriff. She could feel Quinn breathing, fancied the thudding of her heart.

She ran her hands lightly upward, her palms gently following the contours of Quinn's breasts beneath her T-shirt, and as Rachel grazed Quinn's aroused nipples she felt a tremor pass over Quinn's body.

Her hands were shaking slightly as she cupped Quinn's face, kissed her slowly, pulled away. "Your place or mine?" she asked huskily, and Quinn swallowed.

"Yours, I think. I know mine's closer, but yours is bigger. I think we might need the space."

Rachel nibbled on Quinn's lips. "We will?" she breathed against Quinn's mouth.

"Space isn't mandatory, but it's more comfortable."

Rachel could feel Quinn's words against her mouth. Her breasts brushed Quinn's, and her body ignited again. "We'd better go now then, otherwise I won't make it up the stairs."

Quinn laughed softly, a low, sensuous sound that seemed to echo in her chest, her expelled breath playing over Rachel's cheek like cool silk.

"The way I feel right now I could carry you," Quinn said as she clasped Rachel's hand and moved them across the room to the staircase.

"I'll make the climb somehow," Rachel assured her, knowing it wasn't the climb up the stairs that was making her breathless. "I wouldn't want you to waste any of that energy."

They were at the top of the steps now, and Quinn drew Rachel into her arms again, kissed her deeply. Then Rachel was pulling Quinn along the passage and into her bedroom.

The bedside lamp still burned, illuminating the bed with a warm glow, inviting them into its circle of light. They stopped by the bed, moved together, kissed long and languidly, and when they drew apart they were both breathless.

"Well," Quinn said softly. "Last chance."

"To what?" Rachel asked.

Quinn's eyebrow quirked. "To step back. To change your mind."

"My mind was made up a long time ago," Rachel said levelly, her muscles tensing at the naked, sensuous promise in Quinn's eyes.

Quinn reached out, slowly slid Rachel's nightshirt up and over her head, dropping it on the floor, and Rachel stood in her underpants. Suddenly she was shy, wanting to cover herself, wishing there was less of her. She flushed as Quinn's gaze took in her full breasts.

"I guess I'm no Elle Macpherson." She gave a nervous laugh.

Quinn's hands reached out, cupped Rachel's breasts, lifting them slightly, and then her thumbs brushed Rachel's dark nipples.

Rachel's knees gave way beneath her, and she sat down heavily on the side of the bed. Quinn quickly discarded her T-shirt, shorts, and undies. She gently pushed Rachel back onto the bed, peeled off her panties, and stretched her long warm body out beside Rachel's.

"You're just perfect," she said thickly, her eyes drinking in Rachel's naked body.

"Yours is the perfect one. It always was." Her gaze moved over Quinn's small, firm breasts, her rosy nipples, flat midriff and stomach, the shadow of her navel, the tantalizing triangle of dark curls between her long, muscular legs. Quinn *was* quite perfect.

Rachel found it even more difficult to breathe. Her fingers settled on the bare skin of Quinn's stomach, and she had to moisten her dry lips with her tongue. "I want to touch you, but I'm not sure . . . I don't know what to . . . I mean, what you like."

"I like what you like," Quinn replied with a faint smile.

A lump lodged in Rachel's throat. How did she tell Quinn she'd never done this, been with a woman before? "Quinn, I . . ."

Quinn reached out, the back of her hand gently brushing Rachel's cheek, her fingertips settling on Rachel's lips. "I know, Rachel. Just do what you feel, what you'd like to do."

Rachel took Quinn's fingers into her mouth, sucked them, tasted them. Then she raised herself on her elbow and leaned across Quinn to kiss her lips. Rachel's breasts brushed

Quinn's, her nipples tingling, tightening in their arousal, and she gasped as a shaft of pure desire surged through her.

Of their own accord Rachel's fingers moved, settled agitatedly on Quinn's shoulder, slid downward, seeking, arousing, teasing her hardened nipple. Quinn murmured thickly as Rachel's hands caressed her, and Rachel's own body burned, began to throb anew with her own wanting.

Supporting herself on her hands, Rachel slid on top of Quinn, one leg on each side of her hips, and she lowered herself until their bodies meshed. Quinn took one of Rachel's nipples into her mouth, her lips encircling as she gently sucked, teasing with her tongue, her teeth. At the same time her hand enveloped Rachel's other breast, her fingers tantalizing.

A swell of release caught Rachel unawares. Waves of wondrous sensation washed over her, and she relaxed onto Quinn's body. She drew a ragged breath. "I'm sorry. I . . ."

Quinn kissed her tenderly. "Don't apologize. You're wonderful, do you know that?" She gave a soft laugh. "And Elle Macpherson, eat your heart out."

Rachel laughed too, and then Quinn gently pushed against her shoulders, moved her until she was lying on her back again. Quinn leaned across and kissed her deeply, and Rachel couldn't seem to get enough of her soft lips. A flutter of desire rose from deep inside Rachel, began to grow again.

Quinn let her lips move down, teasing Rachel's nipples again, her hand sliding over the small mound of Rachel's stomach, pausing to encircle her belly button. Her magic fingers resumed their journey, fluttered over the inside of Rachel's thighs, touched the tangle of wet pubic curls. And then they were slipping into the damp, inviting folds, finding Rachel's responsive center.

Rachel moaned, heard a voice so unlike her own murmur Quinn's name as Quinn's fingers slid inside her, her thumb gently caressing Rachel's clitoris. Rachel arched against

Quinn's questing fingers, her hands holding Quinn's dark head, keeping Quinn's lips to her breast.

Rachel's body was alive, nerve endings tingling, her arousal clutching at every corner of her being. And when she climaxed again she cried out, her arms crushing Quinn to her, her spasms tugging at Quinn's fingers held deep inside her.

Slowly Rachel's breathing returned to normal, and she realized her cheeks were wet with tears.

Quinn slowly removed her fingers and slid up beside Rachel, kissing her, her fingers brushing at the dampness on Rachel's face. Rachel caught the scent of her arousal on Quinn's hand, and her eyes met Quinn's.

"That was just, well . . ." She paused as her voice broke. "Just indescribable."

Quinn smiled. "I'm glad."

Rachel pulled her close again, kissed her, her hands reaching for Quinn's breasts, fingertips rubbing her nipples.

"I want to . . . Tell me what to do. What you like."

Quinn laughed softly again. "Just what you're doing, for a start." She rolled on her back, and Rachel continued to caress her, delighting in the feel of Quinn's breasts beneath her fingers. She let her hands wander over Quinn's body, filled with wonder at its smoothness, the firm musculature. She paused when she reached Quinn's lower stomach, and she swallowed nervously.

"Rachel?" Quinn's soft voice made Rachel look up at her. "You don't have to do anything you don't want to do, that you're not comfortable with."

Rachel nodded. "I know. It's not that I'm . . . I want to please you too. So much. I'm just unsure, well, how to . . . But I need to."

"Oh, darling," Quinn whispered and reached out to brush Rachel's hair back from her face, one fingertip tracing the line of Rachel's jaw, lingering on her mouth.

Rachel caught her breath. "I want to make love to you very much," she murmured brokenly, and she leaned down, kissed Quinn's flat stomach, drew in the heady scent of Quinn's skin.

With a sigh of pleasure, Rachel's fingers slipped into the wondrous slick warmth between Quinn's legs. She watched Quinn's expression, felt her body's response, caressed her, loved her with her fingers and lips, until Quinn's body spasmed, collapsed against hers.

Rachel shifted up to lie beside Quinn, snuggling close, felt a wondrous oneness with her, their arms and legs entwining as though they had been made to fit together.

"Quinn." Rachel sighed, and Quinn's lips nuzzled her warm cheek. "So beautiful, Quinn." She felt herself smile as she drifted into a deep sleep.

Outside the window the birds were chattering. Sparrows. Must be later, Rachel reflected sleepily, otherwise it would have been the raucous laughing of the kookaburras. She sighed deeply and rolled on her back, her eyes fluttering open to the splash of clear blue sky through the curtains.

It was then she realized she was naked beneath the light sheet, and she turned to glance at the other side of the queen-size bed. She was alone, but the indentation made by Quinn's head on the pillow, the wrinkles of the bedcovers, were proof that Quinn had indeed been there, that the memories that tumbled into Rachel's consciousness had some basis in fact rather than sybaritic fantasy.

Maybe she'd dreamed . . .? No. Last night had been no flight of fancy, no fabrication of her wishful thinking. She and Quinn had made love, made incredible, astonishing, wonderful love. And Rachel knew those moments had changed her whole life.

Her body seemed to hum, and it felt marvelously alive. Each cell, every sinew. She lay there and grinned inanely up at the ceiling, ran her hands lightly over her breasts, her stomach, reliving each electrifying moment, every touch, every murmur. She raised her hands above her head and stretched languidly, feeling the pull in muscles reused.

"You look like the cat that stole the cream," a soft voice said from the doorway.

Chapter Fifteen

Rachel raised herself onto her elbows. "I think I am. And I did," she said, flushing beneath Quinn's hooded gaze.

Quinn came into the room and placed the tray she was carrying on Rachel's bedside table. She was dressed in her discarded T-shirt from the night before. "I was starving, so I thought you would be too. Fancy some of my famous scrambled eggs?"

"Famous?"

Quinn shrugged. "Well, it sounds better than my 'indifferent' scrambled eggs. Where do you want this?" she indicated the tray. "Want to sit up, so I can put the tray on your knees?"

Rachel pushed herself into a sitting position, and the sheet fell away from her breasts, leaving them bare and drawing Quinn's narrowed gaze. Quinn sat down on the side of the bed, leaned across, and slowly licked first one rosy peak and then the other with her warm tongue. Rachel arched toward Quinn's questing lips.

"Mmm. Now that beats the eggs," Quinn said and grimaced. "No pun intended." She turned to lift the tray and set it across Rachel's knees as Rachel giggled.

"Maybe I should put on my nightshirt," Rachel began, and Quinn gave a crooked smile.

"Leave the poor old cook something for her trouble. The scenery here is delightful."

Rachel laughed, lifted her cup of coffee, sipped it, and sighed. She took a few mouthfuls of egg and raised her eyebrows appreciatively. "Definitely 'famous.' And you're right. I'm starving, too."

"Must have been the, um, activity," Quinn teased. "It's supposed to make you ravenous."

Rachel flushed. "I'll have to stock up on provisions then," she said, and Quinn put her hand to her mouth in feigned shock.

"Why, Mrs. Weston. What scandalous behavior."

They laughed together and ate their eggs. Rachel sighed contentedly as she set her coffee mug back on the tray.

"Finished?" Quinn asked. When Rachel nodded, she stood up and returned the tray to the nightstand.

Rachel relaxed against her pillows and smiled at Quinn. "This is five-star service. You know, I've never had breakfast in bed before. It's so decadent."

"Never?"

"No." Rachel shook her head. "Oh, apart from when I was in hospital having the kids. Rob didn't, well, he wasn't very romantic in that way."

Quinn sat back down on the side of the bed, her T-shirt sliding up her smooth thigh, and a spiral of delight clutched low in Rachel's stomach. Quinn took a bite of the piece of the toast she'd smeared with strawberry jam.

Rachel swallowed. Discussing her late husband with Quinn didn't seem right somehow. Not now. "So. Do you make a habit of giving women breakfast in bed?" she asked lightly.

Quinn looked down at her toast for long moments before she met Rachel's gaze. "No. I guess this is a first for me too."

Heavy silence filled the room.

"It is? But . . .?"

"But it wasn't my first time with a woman," she finished, and Rachel flushed again. Quinn sighed. "I guess the general consensus is that women in prison, well . . ." She shrugged. "But I didn't. Not in prison. It was before."

A feeling of dread tore about Rachel's stomach as a vivid picture flashed into her mind, of Laurel Greenwood moving disinterestedly between the colorful rows of plants in the Garden Center as she waited for Quinn. Rachel wanted to change the direction of this conversation, but she didn't know how. "Quinn, you don't have to . . ."

"I know. But I didn't want you to think . . . I wanted you to know the truth." She turned away, returned her half-eaten toast to the tray. She looked back at Rachel. "I knew I was a lesbian when I was about twelve years old. Oh, I didn't exactly have a name for it at the time, I don't think. But I knew I was different." She pulled a face. "Well, even more different than everyone thought I was. But I hid it pretty well." She sighed. "Heaven only knows why when I was so blatantly rebellious about everything else. When all my friends were raving over male pop stars, I was far more interested in their female partners. And I had the usual crushes on women, but they were my secrets. I didn't even tell Laurel about them."

Rachel tried to absorb this disclosure, and for a moment she wondered if Colleen's gossip had been untrue after all. It wasn't Laurel who . . .

"Laurel and I had been going around with Mark and

Graham by then." Quinn picked at a thread on the hem of her T-shirt. "They were friends and Laurel and I were friends, so Laurel decided . . . Well, it seemed like a good idea at the time. But I hated it. I just didn't know what else to do."

Quinn looked back at Rachel. "What about you? With guys?"

Rachel flushed again, feeling indecision clutch at her, her loyalty to Rob warring with her need to be honest with Quinn. "There was only Rob, so I wasn't exactly experienced. But to answer your question, no, I couldn't say I enjoyed it. I mean, it wasn't unpleasant but . . ." Rachel stopped. *But it was nothing like last night*, she wanted to say, yet the words caught in her throat.

"You and Rob. Were you happy?"

"Rob was a good man. He deserved better than me."

"Johnno said Rob was one of the most easygoing guys he'd ever met."

Rachel nodded. "He was certainly laid back. Nothing seemed to get to him. I guess I used to worry for both of us."

"Did he know that you . . .? I mean . . ."

"That I had this secret yearning deep inside me?" Rachel shook her head. "No. No one did. I wouldn't even admit it to myself."

"We all have to find our own way there," Quinn said softly. "It just takes some of us longer than others."

"I guess I was a 'longer than others.' " Rachel took a steadying breath. "And in this town, where everyone knew me, knew my family, it was easier, doing what was expected of me," she finished lamely, feeling as spineless as she sounded.

"I know all about doing what's expected. I know people were scarcely surprised I ended up in jail. But by the time I got out, I'd decided I wanted something different. Maybe you could say I wanted what was expected of everyone else." Quinn hesitated, unconsciously making a negating movement with her head. "Not easy to achieve when you've done time."

"Was it really bad in jail?" Rachel asked.

Quinn unconsciously touched a small scar above her right eye. "I guess it was pretty bad," Quinn said flatly. "I made it worse for myself. I didn't have a hope of getting out when it was time for my first parole hearing." She glanced at Rachel.

"When I first went in, I was half mad. Scared. Confused. Guilty. Angry. You name it. If there was a hard way to do something, that was how I did it. I thought I was literally going insane. I could see myself doing crazy things, but I couldn't seem to stop myself. I even tried to escape. Didn't succeed, of course.

"I'd racked up nearly two years extra on my sentence before I saw this counselor. She was new, and all I remember of that session with her was that she asked me offhandedly if I ever wanted to get out of jail.

"Until that moment I don't think I even considered whether I wanted to get out or not. But everything became crystal clear to me. I don't know. Maybe my life flashed before my eyes or something, but I knew I had to change or I never would get out. Not alive."

Quinn smiled crookedly. "Funnily enough, it was more difficult for me to be a model prisoner than it was to be a hardhead. No one could believe I'd decided to change, least of all my fellow inmates."

She touched the scar above her eye again, and Rachel put her own hand up, ran her finger along the fine ridge. Quinn held Rachel's hand there for long moments. "If one were generous, one would say I got this in a fight for my honor. One day one of the women, a real troublemaker and tough as they come, decided she didn't like her girlfriend talking to me, thought she was two-timing her.

"She started a fight, and then hit the other woman. Then she was kicking her while she was down. I grabbed her to stop her, and they both turned on me. I ended up with this for my trouble.

"They decided it was all my fault, and things got worse.

125

Eventually I was moved for my own safety, and I worked myself out on the farm. Eventually I got my life back."

"I'm grateful you did."

"Me too. I decided to take control of my life. I wanted to, well, try to make up in part for what I'd done. And I wanted a family. I wanted to make something of my life. So I decided to go straight."

She gave a derisive laugh. "In every sense of the word. When I was released, I shared a flat with a woman I'd met at the prison farm. She was a nice woman who'd made some mistakes like I had. She introduced me to her brother, and he was interested in me. He was a nice sort of guy, so I thought, why not?"

Quinn sighed. "Remember when you asked me about Katie's father and I said we didn't love each other enough?"

Rachel nodded.

"That was only part of it. We began our relationship for the wrong reasons. I wanted to prove I could be just like everyone else, and he, well, I'd told him I preferred women, and he told me later he thought he could change me. We were both crying for the moon."

"But you had Katie."

Quinn gave a quick smile. "That we did. And I guess you could say she was the best of both of us. When Doug and I got together, I knew I'd made a mistake pretty well the first night, but I tried to make a go of it. Then one day a couple of months later, he said he'd decided to go down to Adelaide with his sister and her new boyfriend. They'd been promised jobs down there. He didn't ask me to go with them.

"I was relieved. And he left me expecting Katie. I hadn't been trying to get pregnant, but I can't say I wasn't overjoyed. When Katie was born, it made my whole existence seem worthwhile for the first time in my life. Now I don't know what I'd do without her."

Quinn shook her head. "It's strange, isn't it? If things had gone differently before it all happened, who knows what kind of life, what sort of person I'd be now. Where we'd both be."

Rachel wondered that too. She saw Quinn again in the shower block, turning toward her, her towel barely covering her naked body. What if she, Rachel, had stayed that afternoon? What if she'd told Quinn how she felt, that she was attracted to her?

"I suppose it's all relative now," Quinn continued. "I guess I should have known I'd never make a go of it with Doug. My earlier experiences with hetero sex should have told me something."

"It was that bad?" Rachel asked gently, and Quinn nodded.

"It was pretty bad. Physically and emotionally. And looking back, I still can't believe I let Laurel talk me into . . ."

She shook her head. "We'd been going out on double dates with Mark and Graham for a couple of weeks, and Laurel decided it was time we stopped holding them at arm's-length, that it was time we both lost our virginity."

Quinn gave a derisive laugh. "Everyone in town would have been surprised if they'd known we hadn't already but, for all our rebelliousness, we never got into sex. Till that night.

"We were at Laurel's. Her parents were out. The guys came over, and we were drinking. One thing led to another. It was awful. I hated it.

"Afterward, when the guys had left, Laurel and I were in Laurel's room. We decided to take a shower, and she laughingly said we should conserve water, shower together. She seemed to delight in discussing the evening in minute detail, in glowing terms. All I could see were her naked breasts and . . ."

Quinn stood up and walked over to the window. "A couple of days later I came upon an advertisement in a newspaper for a women's information line. I memorized the number, kept repeating it to myself for days before I got up the nerve to make the call."

She sat back against the windowsill, looked across at Rachel. "I poured out everything to the poor woman who answered. Told her how I felt about women. And men. All my fears. She was great. Let me talk it all out. I also stretched the truth, put my age up, told her I was nineteen, and she gave me the numbers for a couple of women's groups. Lesbian groups.

"I rang one, and they gave me some venues. One was a bar, so I figured I'd be at home there." She grimaced. "I went alone, complete with fake ID."

Rachel tried to imagine herself doing something like that back then and knew she wouldn't have had Quinn's courage.

"I met some great women, talked to them. They made me feel as though I wasn't the weirdo I thought I was." Quinn paused. "Actually, I revisited the old haunt the other night after Laurel came to the Garden Center."

So Quinn hadn't been meeting Laurel, as Rachel had surmised. Knowing the truth only made Rachel feel even guiltier for her suspicions.

"But the whole place had changed. Different decor. Different clientele. Nothing stays the same, I guess."

"Did you meet someone special there? When you first went there?" Rachel asked.

Quinn shook her head. "No. Not really. But I made some friends there who made me feel less of a freak." She walked back, sat down on the bed again, picked up Rachel's hand and held it lightly in hers. "After a couple of weeks, Laurel started getting curious about where I was the nights she'd ring and I wasn't home. She teased me about two-timing Graham. I denied it, and she then decided I must be with him. It was easier to let her think that.

"Until she saw Graham somewhere else when I said I was with him. She teased me incessantly, started on again about me seeing another guy, so I told her the truth. I expected her to run screaming with revulsion. But she told me she was interested."

Quinn looked at Rachel. "Interested in me. In that way. That was the beginning. I was half in love with her before, and I wanted us to go away together. She said she loved me too, and she agreed to go with me as soon as we finished school. As long as we kept up the pretense we were just friends. After the accident she changed her mind."

Rachel leaned over and took Quinn in her arms.

"I don't suppose I could have expected anything else. I killed Mark and nearly killed Graham and Laurel. She rang me before the trial to tell me it was over."

"I'm sorry." Rachel kissed Quinn's warm cheek.

Quinn pulled back a little so she could look at Rachel. "At the time I thought she'd broken my heart. But here I am, and it's still beating."

"I can testify to that," Rachel said, moving her hand until it rested on Quinn's breast.

Quinn relaxed back against the bed, pulling Rachel after her. "So what about you, Rachel Weston? What's your story? Why haven't you run off with a gorgeous woman?"

"Maybe I was waiting for you." The words slipped out, and Rachel wasn't sure she'd uttered them until she looked at Quinn. A small frown shadowed the other woman's brow, and Rachel's heart sank. Hadn't last night meant as much to Quinn as it had to her? She gave a quick laugh. "To kiss me awake, like Sleeping Beauty."

Quinn raised a dark eyebrow. "I've never seen myself as anyone's knight in shining armor."

"But you must admit it has a nice ring to it." Rachel touched Quinn's shoulders, one after the other. "Arise, Sir Quinn."

"And what task would my lady ask of me?"

"Ah. I'm sure I could think of something."

"Would this be something I might enjoy?" Quinn asked, her lips struggling not to smile.

Rachel chuckled. "I'm pretty sure you will," she said and ran her fingers over Quinn's breast. "I know I will," she added huskily as she put her lips to Quinn's immediately responsive body.

The phone on the nightstand rang shrilly, and they both jumped. Rachel swore under her breath.

"Don't answer it," Quinn said thickly, and Rachel hesitated.

"It might be —"

"Rose," she finished. Quinn relaxed her grip on Rachel and reached over to pick up the receiver, holding it out to Rachel.

"Rachel Weston."

"Rachel, it's Phil. Sorry to disturb you on your day off, but I've sort of nicked my hand with a broken pot."

"Nicked your . . .? You mean you've cut yourself?" Rachel sat up. "How badly?"

She mimed to Quinn that she was speaking to Phil.

"It's not too bad, but I think I'll need to go up to the hospital and get a stitch or two. I just didn't want to leave Old Dave here on his own."

"Is the cut still bleeding?" Rachel asked. Quinn sat up, a frown on her face.

"Not much."

"Phil, I think you should call an ambulance."

"It's not that bad. Honest," Phil insisted.

"Well, I'm coming right down, and I'll take you to the hospital myself."

"You don't have to do that." Phil paused imperceptibly. "Ah, Ken had just pulled in to pick up those ferns for the MacKenzie job, so he's going to run me up to Casualty. But we'll wait till you get here."

"No, you won't. You go straight to the hospital." It was Rachel's turn to be resolute. "I'll be down there in about twenty minutes. Old Dave can manage till then. Just tell him

130

I'm on my way. And, Phil, get Ken to let me know how things go."

Rachel hung up the phone and turned back to Quinn, filling her in on what had happened.

"God, Quinn, I'm sorry." Rachel picked up Quinn's hand, holding it to her cheek. "I'll have to go."

"I'll come with you."

Rachel shook her head. "No sense in both of us having to go to work on our day off. Besides, we were going up to the farm to see the kids. They're expecting us, so one of us should go."

Quinn hesitated, obviously torn, and Rachel kissed her lingeringly.

"It's okay. I'll phone Fliss and Adam and explain why I can't come too." Rachel slid off the bed. "I'd better have a quick shower and get going."

Quinn's gaze moved over Rachel's naked body. "What a waste," she said huskily and gave Rachel a crooked smile. "I suppose we better not let Phil bleed to death while we . . ." She raised her eyebrows and twirled an imaginary mustache.

Rachel crossed to the *en suite*, turning back to look at Quinn. "Just do one thing for me, hmm?"

Quinn looked across at her.

"Remember exactly where we were up to," she said as she hurried into the shower, Quinn's soft laughter following her.

The next few days passed in a daze for Rachel, a wonderful, exciting, sensual daze. She knew she floated around the Garden Center just waiting for the evening when she could be alone with Quinn.

All day she went through the motions at work, did the things she'd been doing for years. Only now it was so very different.

Now she shared secret smiles with Quinn, touched her surreptitiously as they passed or worked together, her heart racing when she recalled their time alone together, being together, talking, eating, cuddling, making love.

And those times together filled Rachel with a happiness she could never have imagined was possible. Her body, once awakened, surprised her with its response to Quinn's lovemaking. And she delighted in Quinn's body moving so sensuously, so erotically beneath her own touch.

Rachel felt as though the innermost part that was herself, her very essence, had found freedom, had escaped from where she'd buried it so carefully, so deeply within her. And now that it had tasted that freedom, it luxuriated in it, demanding more.

Rachel had caught Phil looking at her inquiringly quite a few times. His hand was duly stitched, and he was on light duties, which kept him closer to the office than usual.

"You look like you've lost twenty cents and found a dollar," he'd teased yesterday, and Rachel had laughed delightedly.

"Found a million dollars, you mean," she said before she could stop herself.

"Ah! I sense a matter of the heart. Who's the lucky winner? Besides you, that is?"

Rachel simply smiled.

"You might as well spill the beans, Rachel. I'll find out eventually."

"I think I'll go over and see how Old Dave's going," Rachel said. "He might need a hand."

"Don't mention that particular part of the body," Phil said in mock horror, nursing his bandaged hand. "And in the interests of public safety, with your heart playing tricks on you, don't even think of driving the loader, Rachel," he added. Rachel walked away laughing.

And now it was Tuesday and Rachel's turn to host their first bridge game of the New Year. She had set up the card table out on the back patio in deference to the heat. The sky was clear and blue, but if the humidity was any indication, they could be in for a tropical thunderstorm later in the day. A light breeze made the back of the house relatively cool, and if it became too hot they could move the game indoors.

Rachel glanced at the sky. As long as there was no hail. Although they were insured, hail could do untold damage to the fragile plants and ruin months of hard work at the Garden Center.

"Just looking at your pool makes me feel cooler," said Rhonda later as they broke for lunch. "Wish I'd brought my swimsuit."

"I have spares if you want to take a dip," Rachel told her. She placed the sandwiches Quinn had helped her make for lunch on the side table.

"I just might take you up on that after the game," Rhonda said as she put some food on her plate. "If I don't eat too much. These look very more-ish, Rachel."

Sandy bit into a sandwich. "Mmm. They're scrumptious. Is that cream cheese?"

"Light cream cheese for our waistlines." Rachel patted her stomach. "Mixed with pineapple juice and shaved ham and some of Rose's mango chutney."

"These aren't bad either." Colleen looked at the filling in her own sandwich.

"Apricots, walnuts, chicken, and mayonnaise."

Colleen raised her eyebrows at Rachel. "Delicious. Where did you get the recipes?"

Rachel gave her attention to choosing her own sandwich. "Actually, from Quinn. She helped me make them. For a few months before Katie was born, she worked in a gourmet sandwich shop. These are a couple of their recipes."

Colleen's eyes narrowed. "Mum told me Quinn Farrelly was renting your unit."

"Yes." Rachel took a sip of her fruit juice. "It fits in really well. We carpool when we're on the same shifts."

"I take it Quinn's working today?" Rhonda asked.

133

"I suppose Quinn's sister looks after her little girl, does she?" asked Sandy.

"Quinn's sister-in-law was looking after Katie, but Josie's gone down to the coast for a week or two, so Katie's going to Cindy with Fliss and Adam."

"I thought Cindy had measles or something?" Colleen chose another mouth-watering sandwich.

"Chicken pox." Rachel drew a quick breath. "So Katie's gone with my kids up to the farm until next week when they go back to Cindy. It worked out well. I'm just glad they could stay with Rose and Charlie."

Colleen paused with her sandwich halfway to her mouth. "You seem to have got very chummy with Quinn Farrelly."

Rachel could almost laugh at that. Chummy? If Colleen only knew. A picture of Quinn's smooth naked body moving over her own the evening before made Rachel's pulse rate increase. What would her cousin say if she told her exactly how close she and Quinn had become?

She made herself shrug as casually as she could. "I guess we have."

Three pairs of eyes regarded her levelly, and Rachel couldn't prevent herself from flushing.

"Quinn's, well, fun to be with."

"Fun to be with?" Colleen exclaimed. "She's an ex-con."

Rachel took a steadying breath. "With the emphasis on the *ex*," she said evenly.

"You're a hard woman, Col," chastised her sister. "It's all old news now. People grow older, change."

"I'm not so sure people like Quinn Farrelly can change." Colleen remarked, her tone darkly ominous.

"Sandy's right," agreed Rhonda. "What's the point in dredging it all up again?"

"Quinn's bright and, well," Rachel paused. "She's great at work. She loves her daughter and she, well, she makes me laugh."

As Rachel added the last bit, she realized how true that

was. Most of the time they spent together they were laughing. When they weren't making love. Rachel quickly pushed that dangerous thought aside. It wouldn't do for Colleen to pick up on that, and Rachel knew from past experience how astute her cousin could be.

Yes, Quinn made Rachel laugh, and Rachel realized she'd never been happier. Did she have to sacrifice that happiness because social conventions dictated she couldn't love another woman?

"I'll just get the coffee to have with dessert. Pavlova, if anyone's interested," Rachel said lightly, and there were murmurs of approval.

Inside, Rachel took a few moments to settle her breathing. It was exhausting keeping up this subterfuge. If Quinn had been a man, Rachel would have eagerly told her friends about the new love in her life. And her friends would have questioned her just as excitedly. If they discovered her relationship with Quinn, would they be accepting or appalled?

And her children. What would be the consequences for Fliss and Adam? They were her children, and she loved them dearly. She'd tried to teach them tolerance, but when it came down to everyday life, were they old enough to take such monumental changes in their stride?

Rachel saw her life whirling into dangerous, uncharted waters. Would she be strong enough to get through it?

And what was the alternative? she asked herself. To give up Quinn?

Rachel's heart ached. How could she do that now, after . . .? Wouldn't it be simpler to carry on a secret affair? Then no one need know. No one would have to decide one way or the other.

Rachel mechanically went about brewing coffee and assembling the pavlova, adding cream and fresh fruit, mango, banana, kiwi fruit, pawpaw, and passionfruit.

Of course it was all relative, Rachel reminded herself as waves of churning, self-doubt engulfed her. She didn't know what Quinn thought about their relationship. Rachel knew she was in love with Quinn, but was Quinn as involved as Rachel was? What if she wasn't? Maybe Quinn didn't want . . .?

Carefully picking up the pavlova, Rachel walked toward the door.

"I don't know why you're so worried, Colleen. Rachel deserves to have a good time."

Rachel paused at her cousin Sandy's words.

"Yes." Rhonda concurred. "All she's done since Rob died is work and raise the kids."

"I'm not saying Rachel shouldn't have some relaxation time," Colleen continued. "All I'm concerned about is what sort of fun Quinn Farrelly might be interested in."

"As Sandy said, Quinn's older and hopefully wiser. You can't judge her on the past, Colleen. She was just a kid. And, apart from that, Rachel's no fool. She's not going to do anything, well, silly. "

"I know that. It's not Rachel I'm concerned about exactly. I just wouldn't want her involved with a beer-swilling, anti-establishment lesbian."

A moment of silence followed Colleen's words.

"Lesbian?" Rhonda repeated.

"You think Quinn still drinks?" Sandy asked at the same time.

"Who knows?"

"Exactly, Col." Sandy put in. "We don't know. But if she is a lesbian . . . Well, Rachel's not a lesbian."

Rachel stood stock-still, part of her wishing she could simply walk out and tell them the truth. Which was? she asked herself ruthlessly. That she'd always preferred the company of women. That she'd always had a secret yearning for a woman. For one particular woman. And that she was now hopelessly in love with that woman. Emotionally and physically. If that made her a lesbian, then that's what she was.

"I know Rachel's not a lesbian," Colleen was saying. "But does Quinn Farrelly know that?"

"I've never believed you can turn someone gay, be it a man or a woman," Rhonda stated. "You either are or you aren't."

"What about people who are bisexual?" Sandy almost whispered.

"Maybe they're just confused," replied Rhonda.

"Let's just hope Rachel doesn't get confused."

"Don't be ridiculous, Col. Rachel's the most sensible person I know. She wouldn't, well . . . But if she did, or was, it wouldn't make any difference to me. And it shouldn't matter to you. Now, I'm going to help Rachel with the coffee." Sandy's chair squeaked as she stood up, and Rachel took a step back into the kitchen and waited for her cousin to appear.

The next afternoon Rachel sat in her office and began going through the mail.

She hadn't mentioned the conversation she'd overheard yesterday to Quinn because . . . Because? Why hadn't she? she asked herself. It could have been quite amusing. They could have laughed over it. Couldn't they?

Rachel sighed. She knew she hadn't mentioned the contents of the conversation to Quinn because she was unsure about how Quinn saw their relationship. She admitted she was simply closing her mind to everything except the enjoyment of the moment.

But she knew she'd have to face her own questions sooner rather than later. The three children would be returning at the weekend, and Rachel knew she and Quinn couldn't continue to have the freedom they were relishing at the moment with the house to themselves. They were going to have to talk about it. Make some decisions.

Rachel pushed her disquieting thoughts to the back of her mind and slit open a large pink envelope. She read the invitation with extremely mixed feelings.

"Caught you!" Phil exclaimed from the doorway. "Pink envelope. Must be a love letter." He turned to grin at Quinn, who had walked up to the office with him. "The boss has got a beau."

Rachel's eyes met Quinn's, and Rachel felt herself flush. "Sorry to disappoint your romantic little heart, Phil, but it's just an invitation. To Rachel Weston and staff, that would include you two, to attend a reception for Mike Greenwood's acceptance to run for state office, etc, etc. Four tickets. Formal. For Friday." Rachel held out the invitation, and Phil took it from her.

If the reception was for Mike Greenwood, then no doubt his wife would be there. Rachel wasn't sure how she felt about that, but she suspected what she did feel seemed to be bordering on jealousy. Which was ridiculous, she told herself. One simple question to Quinn would solve that problem.

But what if Quinn . . .?

"The formal's a bit of a downer," Phil was saying, "but it says here free food and drink, if I'm not mistaken. What say I round up Ken and we all go together? Unless you want to ask this new man along, Rachel?"

"I told you, there is no new man," Rachel said quickly, avoiding looking at Quinn.

"Sounds like it might be something you should go to, business-wise," Quinn said casually, and Phil nodded his agreement.

"Quinn's right. These things are where big deals are done."

"I hardly think everyone is going to be standing with their wineglasses, waiting eagerly to buy truckloads of plants," Rachel said wryly.

Phil chuckled. "Who knows? But you won't have to cook dinner, and there'll be the scintillating conversation of your escorts."

"How can we refuse such an offer, Rachel?" Quinn laughed. "With such handsome men on our arms, we'll be the envy of the entire populace."

"Couldn't have put it better myself," Phil said with satisfaction. "I'll arrange it with Ken." He looked at the invitation again. "We'll collect you at, what? Seven?"

Chapter Sixteen

Quinn wore dark slacks and a white collarless shirt, the long sleeves folded back halfway between her wrist and her elbow. Over the shirt she had on a dark tailored waistcoat, the front a rich maroon brocade.

Her dark hair sat neatly in place, swept back from the sides of her head, strands from the top falling nonchalantly over her forehead. And she almost took Rachel's breath away.

In those few moments after the door to the unit opened and Rachel turned to see Quinn standing there, Rachel quite literally forgot to breathe. Looking into Quinn's eyes, Rachel knew she was so deeply in love with this beautiful woman there was no way she could ever go back.

Rachel reached out to her, her hand brushing the

smoothness of Quinn's cheek, the swell of her breast, her fingers fumbling to undo the top buttons of Quinn's shirt, and she heard Quinn's own breath catch in her throat.

"I have this irresistible urge to kiss you right there, between your beautiful breasts," Rachel said huskily and proceeded to do so. Then she groaned softly and buttoned Quinn's shirt. "If I don't stop now, I won't be able to."

"And I won't want you to." Quinn drew Rachel into her arms, held her close. "My God! Your perfume, it's intoxicating," she said and Rachel laughed a little breathlessly.

"It's you that's intoxicating, my darling Quinn."

At that moment the blast of Phil's car horn cut inconsiderately between them.

Quinn placed a quick, teasing kiss on Rachel's eager lips. "Saved by the horn, I'd say."

"Well, I'm not so sure that good timing was really so good, are you?" Rachel reached up and wiped a smudge of her light lipstick from Quinn's lips, and Quinn caught Rachel's fingers in her mouth, nibbled on them playfully.

A loud rat-a-tat sounded on the door, and Quinn gave Rachel a rueful grimace before turning her and pushing her gently in the direction of the door.

Rachel smoothed her hair nervously and checked the fall of her one and only cocktail dress before opening the door.

Phil Stevens gave a soft, drawn-out whistle, his gaze going admiringly from Rachel to Quinn and back to Rachel. "Wow! Don't you two scrub up well."

"How crass can you get, mate?" Ken Leeson admonished Phil as he joined him on the patio. "Don't you have a way with words? Scrub up well, I ask you."

"As a matter of fact, I could say the same for you two." Quinn laughed. "Those suits and dress shirts are a far cry from your usual Garden Center uniforms."

And Rachel had to admit that both men looked extremely handsome.

Phil held up his hands in surrender, the white bandage on

his left hand in stark contrast to his dark suit jacket. "Before we all get into trouble, let's just say that we all look like a million dollars and that we're worthy representatives of the town's most successful and flourishing garden and landscaping business."

"It's the only garden and landscaping business," said Rachel dryly.

"There's that plant nursery on Carver Road," Ken put in helpfully.

"Ah. I'd forgotten about that."

"Ours is better," stated Phil.

Quinn laughed. "Without a doubt."

"Now that we've got that settled . . ." Phil glanced at his watch. "Time to go."

"Are you all right driving with your wounded hand?" Rachel asked.

"Just have to be careful when I change gears." Phil flexed his hand. "Okay, let's go get the free food and champers. We'll need it to block out the political speak that you can bet will be flying around tonight."

"Anyone would think he didn't want to go," Quinn remarked as they walked down to Phil's car.

"Take no notice of him," Ken said as he opened both passenger side doors.

Rachel found herself in the front with Phil while Quinn sat in the back with Ken. Had Ken maneuvered the seating arrangements so that Quinn sat with him? Rachel felt a mixture of emotions churn away inside her, but she made herself block them out. It wasn't as though this was a date or anything. Rachel tried to quash her misgivings. They were all simply going together to represent the business.

Not that it looked that way, Rachel admitted. To all outward appearances they were two women being escorted by two very handsome men, and Rachel hoped Colleen didn't get to hear about it. She'd never let Rachel forget it. And Sandy would be over the moon. She'd been trying to match-make Rachel with Phil for ages.

Rachel swallowed a shiver of disquiet. Of course Colleen would get to hear about this evening. It was the stuff small-town gossip thrived on. She just hoped they weren't fabricating more problems for themselves.

"Phil will always go where there's free food," Ken was continuing.

"Fair go, mate. You make it sound like I make a habit of freeloading," Phil replied, sounding highly affronted as he pulled out onto the road.

"What about that do at the Lions Club last week?"

"Well, I was invited. It would have been rude to refuse." Phil frowned. "Apart from that, I was interested in the subject. And I didn't see you knock back sustenance, as I recall."

Rachel shot a sideways look at Phil as he drove toward the town center. She knew little about Phil's private life even though they were related by marriage. Phil had always seemed a very private person, and although Rachel knew that Phil and Ken spoke to each other at work, she was surprised to hear they apparently knew each other socially.

"Was that the meeting arranged by the local Greenies?" Quinn asked easily, and Ken nodded.

"That was the one. There's a lot of concern about the rumors the Council plans on selling off some designated parklands. And the food aside, Phil's right. It was a really interesting evening. You should have come along."

"The Council needs watching," Phil said, warming to the subject. "Old man Greenwood would sell the mayoral robes if he thought he could get away with it."

The Convention Center of the City Hall was ablaze with lights, and Phil turned into the car park, grumbling as they had to drive around for a few minutes before they found a parking space.

"I was almost ready to say, I told you we should have taken

143

a taxi." Ken laughed as they climbed from the car and headed toward the entrance.

Once inside Rachel glanced around her, surprised at the size of the crowd at the reception.

"Well," Phil said softly for her ears only. "It's obvious anyone who's anybody is here tonight."

Rachel saw the mayor, Laurel's father-in-law, right away. He was a tall, distinguished looking man, and he stood at the center of a group of his fellow councilors, an arm around the shoulders of his equally tall son.

Mike Greenwood had grown from the good looking teenager Rachel remembered into an extremely attractive man. His dark hair was flecked with gray at the temples. Premature gray surely, Rachel reflected. Mike would be, what? Thirty-seven or eight. He had been a year or so older than Rob, so he must be all of that.

Rachel's gaze moved around the rest of the room, and she saw Laurel Greenwood standing at the bar. As Rachel watched, Laurel took a hearty gulp of the drink the barman set in front of her.

From this distance Laurel looked poised and sophisticated. She wore a black sheath that reached her ankles and the slit up the side of the skirt to her mid-thigh showed off her shapely legs. The bodice hugged her full breasts, and shoestring straps nestled over her creamy shoulders.

Rachel glanced at Quinn and knew instinctively that Quinn was watching Laurel as well. But Quinn's expression gave away none of her thoughts.

"That's a nice dress the divine Mrs. G is almost wearing," said Phil as he took a glass of bubbly from a passing waiter.

"If you've got it, flaunt it." Ken laughed. "And having an attractive wife won't hurt Mike Greenwood's political aspirations, that's for sure."

Just then Laurel looked up from her drink and saw their group. She began to thread her way in their direction, stopping occasionally to smile and chat to some members of the crowd.

"So glad you could make it," she said a little breathily when she reached them.

Rachel saw Laurel's eyes go to Quinn, lashes fluttering as she smiled at the other woman.

"We heard the food would be delicious," Phil quipped outrageously, and Laurel turned her gaze on him, her eyes admiring him.

"I don't think you'll have any reason to complain," Laurel said huskily, holding his gaze, and Rachel noted a slight flush color Phil's neck.

"My father-in-law always uses these caterers for his business functions, so they come well recommended." Laurel turned her attention to Rachel, that same false smile lifting the corners of her perfect mouth. "You must let me introduce you to George, Rachel. The council often subcontracts parks and gardens work. It might be worth your while."

Rachel wanted to tell Laurel that she had already supplied plants for the council, but at that moment Mike Greenwood joined his wife.

"There you are, darling," he said, sliding a possessive arm around her, his hand cupping the swell of her hip. He made a show of kissing his wife on the forehead, and Laurel leaned against him.

They made an attractive couple, Rachel acknowledged, Mike so tall and dark, Laurel so petite and fair.

"You might remember Rachel Weston, darling, from schooldays, although she was actually one of my teachers." Laurel turned her false smile in Rachel's direction again.

Her husband frowned, and Rachel could tell he had absolutely no recollection of her. She made herself hold out her hand.

"I was Rachel Richardson, but I was quite a few years behind you."

"Rachel owns a garden center, the one out on Ritchie Road," Laurel explained.

"Oh yes. I think I've passed it," Mike said noncommittally.

"And this is . . ." Laurel flapped her hand and gave the

men an apologetic look that said she was sorry she couldn't recall their names.

"Phil Stevens." Phil shook Mike Greenwood's hand. "And Ken Leeson. We both work for Rachel. And Quinn . . ."

"You remember Quinn?" Laurel took over again. "Quinn Farrelly. Quinn and I were in the same class at school."

Mike Greenwood's eyes narrowed as they moved over Quinn. "Oh yes. I heard you were out."

There was a tense second or so of silence.

"Actually, I've been back," Quinn paused slightly, pointedly holding Mike Greenwood's gaze, "a while now," she finished evenly, although she didn't offer to shake hands with Laurel's husband.

"Well, darling." Mike gazed down at his wife. "Dad wants to introduce you to some of his cronies from interstate." He flashed a charming smile at Phil and Ken. "I'm afraid I'll have to steal my gorgeous wife away."

Laurel smiled as Mike turned her around and they headed back across the room.

"Prick!" muttered Phil and grabbed the attention of another passing waiter, a young man he appeared to know. "Hi, Greg. Bring those drinks over here so we can take them off your hands." He put his empty glass on the tray and handed out glasses of champagne to each of them. He took a sip and inclined his head in the direction of Laurel and Mike. "Those two are welcome to each other."

Rachel glanced across at Quinn, but the other woman was giving her untouched glass of champagne her full attention.

"Sorry about that, Quinn. Greenwood's a rude bastard. And if Ken and I wore gloves we'd slap his face with one and challenge him to twenty paces at dawn," Phil stated.

Quinn smiled. "Thank you, kind sir. But I hardly think he's worth having to ride your horses to the coast and hop a leaking freighter across the Tasman to escape the avenging posse."

"To New Zealand. Now there's a thought." Phil grinned

and then sobered. "Do you find many people like him? Who toss up your past, I mean?"

Quinn shrugged. "On and off. Although few with less manners than he has."

"Whatever he's running for, he just lost my vote," Ken said.

They moved into the room and were soon drawn into the noisy crowd. Rachel noticed Quinn give her untouched glass of champagne back to a waiter in exchange for a fruit juice before she disappeared into the throng of people.

Rachel was soon greeted by various business acquaintances, and she completely lost sight of the other three. And she was finding it more than a little difficult keeping up with the conversations as she found herself continually looking for Quinn in the crowded convention center.

A whole gambit of conflicting emotions vied for supremacy inside her. She felt like her contradictory feelings battled with her innate need to be honest about herself. She wanted to tell everyone how she felt about Quinn, and yet she wanted to hug the secret to herself.

In an ideal world she would be able to declare herself a lesbian, but she knew this was not an ideal world, and this knowledge bade her be cautious. She had two children to protect, her family to consider, and she had to continue running a business in this town.

"Hello, Rachel."

She turned to face Steve Stevens. "Hi, Steve. I'm surprised to see you here."

He grinned crookedly, looking very much like his brother. "And I was just as surprised when Phil told me you were here. However, here we are."

"Do you know the Greenwoods?" Rachel asked.

"I did some work for Mike's company, and I hope to do a bit more, so . . ." He shrugged philosophically.

Rachel grinned. "Say no more."

"It's not my cup of tea, though." He ran a finger around the collar of his shirt. "All this standing about in a monkey suit trying to make conversation with people, some of whom I scarcely know. But Sandy wanted to come. It's more her scene, I'm afraid."

Rachel looked around and spied her cousin nearby. That ensured Colleen would get to hear all about the evening. Sandy waved and made her way across to them.

"I can't believe this place is so packed," she said as she slipped her arm through her husband's. "How come you didn't mention you were coming when we played bridge on Tuesday, Rachel?"

"I, we decided to come at the last minute," Rachel replied lamely.

"I wouldn't have even known it was on if I hadn't found the invitation in one of Steve's shirts he put in the wash." She gave Steve's arm a shake.

Steve grinned at Rachel. "Guess it just slipped my mind."

"Humph! That's what you tell me. I still say you hid the invitation." Sandy looked around. "There are stacks of well known people here. I even saw that newsreader, the one on channel nine. And the press is having a field day. I'm nearly blinded by the camera flashes."

Suddenly Quinn materialized beside them, and Rachel felt a surge of pleasure.

"Managed to fight my way to the food tables," she said as she passed Rachel a plate of hors d'oeuvres. "Thought you might be hungry," she added softly, momentarily holding Rachel's gaze.

Rachel's nerve endings tingled. *Starving for you.* She gathered herself together and made the introductions.

"How about a fresh drink?" Quinn asked.

Rachel looked at her empty glass. "Well . . ."

Quinn grinned and took the glass from her. She turned to Sandy and Steve. "Can I get you two a refill?"

"Please." Sandy smiled at her. "Fruit juice for me, and a light beer for Steve."

Quinn nodded and was lost in the crowd.

"My god, Rachel! Quinn looks great," Sandy stated when Quinn had left them. "I've always coveted dark hair."

Steve turned to look bewilderedly at his wife. "Aren't you always getting your hair blonded? And what about the old saying about gentlemen preferring blondes?"

"That's a myth," Sandy assured him. "Gentlemen prefer any woman who looks like Quinn Farrelly. Don't you think so, Rachel?"

Rachel held up her hand. "Don't ask me questions like that, Sandy. I've got no idea what gentlemen prefer."

"Mmm." Sandy regarded her cousin seriously. "It's time you did notice, but I'm not going to pressure you, Rachel, because at least you've taken the first step."

"I have?" Rachel laughed. "What step is that?"

"Getting out. And that dress really suits you." She looked sharply at Rachel's flushed face, her glowing eyes. "You look, well, wonderful. Doesn't she, Steve?"

"You look wonderful, Rachel," echoed Steve.

Rachel burst out laughing. "You've learned your lines well."

"Oh no. I mean it, Rachel," Steve started to reassure her, looking slightly embarrassed.

Sandy shushed him. "She's teasing you, Steve. I ran into Phil a while ago, and I was also pleased when he told me you came with him tonight."

"Well, we . . . He kindly gave me a lift." Rachel flushed, and Sandy grinned knowingly. "It's not what you think, Sandy. And I told you I don't mix business with pleasure." And how was that different with Quinn? a relentless little voice inside her asked, but she brushed the thought aside. "We, that is, Phil and Ken and Quinn and I, came in Phil's car because we were all coming to the reception tonight."

"A likely story." Sandy quipped.

"What's a likely story?" asked Quinn as she rejoined them and handed out the drinks.

"Rachel's been trying to tell me that you two just got a lift with Phil and Ken, two of the most attractive and eligible men in the room."

Quinn paused, her drink halfway to her lips. And Rachel couldn't seem to drag her gaze from Quinn's mouth. Those wonderful lips.

"Rachel's right, I'm afraid, Sandy," Quinn said solemnly. "Sad state of affairs, isn't it?"

"Doesn't sound sad to me," stated Steve. "My brother can be a total bore when he gets on his pet subjects."

Sandy gave him a quelling look. "All men are like that," she said. "It's one of the crosses we women have to bear."

Just then someone claimed Sandy and Steve's attention, and Rachel found herself alone with Quinn, caught in the crowd.

Quinn fanned her face with her hand. "Wow! It's so hot in here, even with the air conditioning. How about some fresh air?"

Rachel nodded. "That would be wonderful but . . ." She looked around at the closed doors out onto the veranda.

"Is that Japanese Garden still around the side of the building?"

"They dug it up last year," Rachel told her. "Had some trouble with some of the trees, so it's not Japanese any more, just your usual garden variety garden."

"What say we step outside and you show me," Quinn said and ran her hand along the inside of Rachel's lower arm.

Rachel's skin burned at the touch. She'd just turned in the direction of the doors when Quinn's brother joined them.

"Evening, Rachel. Can I borrow Quinn for a few moments? I want to introduce her to some people from my company."

"Of course," Rachel said quickly, her heart sinking.

Quinn rolled her eyes. "Must we, Johnno?"

"Call it family duty." Johnno laughed.

Quinn held Rachel's gaze. "I won't be long." She looked over to the doors. "See you later."

Rachel watched them move away. Did Quinn mean they would still meet outside? She sighed. Well, she could do with the fresh air anyway. She walked across and slipped out through the door.

Quite a few other people were already on the veranda, and some had seated themselves on the benches on the lawn. She caught sight of Phil and Ken talking to a group of people as she wandered along the veranda.

The garden Quinn spoke of was well lit by strategically placed, old-fashioned style lampposts that had replaced the Japanese lanterns. Rachel found an unoccupied bench off to the side. She should be able to see Quinn when she came along either of the two paths between the young bushes.

Some time later, when she'd disappointedly decided she may as well go back inside, she caught sight of Quinn striding along the far pathway that led to a newly erected pergola.

Rachel stood up, went to call Quinn's name, but she paused, smiled to herself. If she continued along this path, it would converge with the path Quinn had taken. They would meet at the pergola. Before she could have second thoughts, Rachel started following the path to intercept Quinn.

Her shoes made little noise on the pavers, and she heard voices before she reached the curve in the path that led to the pergola. Rachel hesitated, walked quietly along until she could see the two figures standing under the pale glow of the overhead lamp.

There was no mistaking the burnished blond hair that glistened in the artificial light. Rachel instinctively drew back against a bush, trying to decide what to do. Her first impulse was to turn back the way she'd come, leave Quinn and Laurel to their conversation, but . . .

"How can you say that, Quinn?" Laurel pleaded. "After all we meant to each other."

Chapter Seventeen

Rachel froze, telling herself she should give the other two some indication she was there. But something made her shrink farther back into the concealing shrubbery.

"Laurel, please. This is a public place. Someone will hear you."

"I don't care," Laurel exclaimed petulantly.

"Well, I *do* care," Quinn stated.

Laurel laughed. "That's not the Quinn I used to know."

"And that's the point, Laurel. You *don't* know me any more."

"I can't believe you could have changed that much."

"Would it be so unusual? It has been twelve years, Laurel.

Now, this isn't the time or place for this conversation. Go on back to the reception. Your husband will miss you."

"He won't miss me the way you mean. I'm just a possession to him, a beautiful doll to show off to his mates." Laurel moved closer to Quinn, reached out, and touched her arm. "I never cared about Mike, Quinn. You know that. It was always you."

Rachel's breath caught in her throat. She shouldn't be eavesdropping. She had no right . . .

"I don't want to hear this," Quinn said firmly. "You're twelve years too late. And apart from that, you have a very selective memory. Or have you conveniently forgotten what you said back then?"

"My parents made me tell you I never wanted to see you again. But I did, Quinn. I really did. They never left me alone, day or night. I couldn't get away."

"Oh sure. Well, it's all relative now, so I see no point in us rehashing the past."

Rachel hovered on the path, knowing she should leave, but unable to do so.

"What if I said I still love you?"

Quinn gave a bitter laugh. "And what would you have me say to that? Let's run away together, leave this town behind us, set up house?"

"We wouldn't have to. We could, well, see each other."

"See each other?" Quinn laughed harshly again. "You mean sneak around for the occasional clandestine roll in the hay?"

"I seem to remember you used to enjoy our secret trysts, no matter where we did it."

Rachel didn't hear Quinn's low reply.

"No one need know." Laurel appealed. "No one did before."

"I'm not interested in a dishonest, furtive affair."

"I think you're protesting too much, Quinn. Remember how exciting it was, how turned on we used to get?"

"Laurel, we were kids."

"I know. And I know we almost got caught once." She giggled. "Remember, Quinn? If Mr. James had come along a few minutes earlier, he'd have caught us in the act, so to speak."

"Well, I was never convinced he didn't see anything. People looked at us differently after that."

"Don't be silly. No one suspected a thing. And they still won't. Everyone knows we're friends from way back. Mike's away a lot, and I have a nanny for the boys."

"I have a child too, Laurel. And a job I don't want to lose."

Laurel gave a low laugh. "Oh, I'm sure Rachel would give you time off. You were always the teacher's pet. And given half the chance, I'd say you could have been more than that to proper Miss Richardson."

Rachel felt her cheeks burn at Laurel's comment.

"Leave Rachel out of this, Laurel." Quinn said coldly.

"You know, I think you still have a teensy little crush on her."

"Laurel . . ."

"Well, you did have a crush on her." Laurel paused. "Maybe you still have."

"You're being ridiculous."

"Am I? Do you still have the hots for her, Quinn? And working with her all day, living in her house, how convenient. Is that why you don't want me any more? Is our prissy old teacher warming your bed?"

"I don't want to hear any of this, Laurel. Go back inside."

"Oh, Quinn, don't be like that. I know Rachel's as straight as they come. I was just teasing you."

"I don't get the joke. And I don't care to talk to you tonight, so go on back to your party."

"You never used to be so cruel, Quinn."

"Leave it, Laurel. Please."

"I love you, Quinn. I always have. You can't send me away. Oh, darling." There was a shuffling noise, and Laurel moaned.

Something twisted inside Rachel as she watched Laurel fold herself against Quinn's stiff body. And then Quinn was deliberately putting Laurel away from her.

"Stop it, Laurel. You're drunk."

"I'm not nearly drunk yet."

"You reek of it."

"You think this is drunk? I'll have you know I could always hold my liquor better than you could. Remember?"

"Remember! You're missing the point, Laurel. All I want to do is forget."

"If it's forgetting you want, then have some of my beer." She held up the long-necked stubbie. "It'll take the edge off, and pretty soon you won't even know you've forgotten anything."

"I don't drink any more."

Laurel giggled. "Don't drink. Don't smoke. Please don't tell me you don't go out with wild women."

Quinn didn't reply.

"So, what do you do?" Laurel asked and ran her finger over the front of Quinn's waistcoat. "And who with?"

Quinn took hold of her hand and turned the other woman around. "Come on, I'll walk you back to the party."

"No." Laurel stepped back under the pergola. "I want to party here. With you. Just the two of us."

Rachel could see Quinn looking at Laurel, and she took a steadying breath, staying perfectly still. If she tried to leave now Quinn would see her movement, would realize Rachel had overheard their conversation.

"You said the same thing that night." Laurel's voice was low and husky. "Let's get out of here, you said. Let's go somewhere and party. Just the two of us."

"That night?" Quinn repeated.

"Yes. *That* night." Laurel took another gulp of her drink. "The night everything went wrong. The car. The crash. It was Graham who said to take the road by the creek. Graham, your boyfriend. He wanted to stop on the riverbank, make love with me. Men are absolute bastards, Quinn. He said you and Mark were too drunk to even notice. Well, we stopped all right."

"Graham? Graham said to take River Road?" Quinn asked slowly, and Laurel sat down on the wooden bench.

"Come sit beside me, Quinn." She tapped the seat, spilling some of her beer on her dress.

"Laurel, when did Graham tell you he said that?"

"He didn't tell me. I knew. I was there too, if you remember."

"You remember . . .?" Quinn sat down heavily on the seat. "They said you only recalled getting into the car, and nothing after that."

"It was the only way I could get them off my back. My parents. The police. Oh, everyone. They kept at me. Pressured me. I wanted it to stop."

"I don't remember any of it," Quinn said softly.

"I know." Laurel leaned against Quinn. "When one of the nurses told me that, I decided to tell them what they wanted to hear."

"What they wanted to hear? What do you mean?"

"I don't want to talk about it any more. It upsets me." Laurel held up her drink. "We're supposed to be partying. Have a drink, Quinn. One won't hurt you. For old times sake."

Quinn grabbed Laurel's arm. "Tell me what happened that night, what you remember."

"Quinn! You're hurting me."

Rachel watched as Quinn seemed to make herself relax, but she didn't let go of Laurel's arm.

"Laurel, tell me about that night."

"I don't want to. I don't think about it. Have a drink, Quinn. It'll make you forget too."

"Forget killing Mark? Maiming Graham? And you?" Quinn ran her hand through her hair. "How can I forget? I have nightmares about it. I live through it over and over."

"You do?" Laurel shook her head, as though she was trying to clear it. "Then why didn't you tell them the truth? About what really happened?"

A portentous silence seemed to hold time suspended. Some small detached part of Rachel felt the prickle of the bush she was pressed against, recognized the perfume of a flowering frangipani nearby. But the rest of her paused, as she knew instinctively Quinn hesitated, her brain processing Laurel's words, not daring to believe what might be behind Laurel's inebriated ramblings.

"You told them I was driving," Quinn said flatly.

"I only told them what they'd already decided. I mean, they were talking about it at the hospital, outside my room. How you were always in trouble. They just took it for granted you were driving."

"I wasn't, was I, Laurel?"

The skin on Rachel's bare arms goose-bumped at Quinn's tone.

"You were too drunk."

"Then who *was* driving?"

Laurel gulped at her drink. "I told you. I don't want to talk about it any more. I feel sick."

"Tell me, Laurel. Don't I deserve the truth?"

"Don't you see, Quinn? Everyone just expected it of you. You'd been in trouble before. You were always in trouble. I couldn't see how it would make any difference to your life. But I, well, my parents expected so much more of me. Yours didn't care . . ."

"You told them I was driving when it was you. Wasn't it, Laurel? It was you?"

"They'd already decided it was you. I didn't see how it would matter. And later, when they told me about Mark, well, it was too late. You see, Quinn?"

"I wasn't driving." Quinn stood up, paced across the wooden deck of the pergola. She spun around, faced Laurel.

"God, Laurel! All these years you knew. How could you let me think . . .?"

"It just, well, happened. What should I have done, Quinn? Suddenly said I was mistaken? Should I have told them to let you go? Take me to jail instead? I'd have died, locked up in prison for years. You were so much stronger than I was. I knew you'd be all right."

Quinn gazed down at the other woman. "But Graham made a statement too. He said . . ."

Laurel stood up, swayed slightly. "I told him not to tell the police anything."

"I can't understand why Graham agreed to do it."

"Mark had told me they, Mark and Graham, had broken into some houses, stolen money and stuff. Mark even gave me a ring he'd taken. So I told Graham I'd tell the police about that if he didn't keep quiet. He agreed, and he left town right afterward. I haven't seen him since."

Quinn rubbed a trembling hand over her face, pinched the bridge of her nose.

"We were found together," Laurel continued in a flat voice, as though once started she couldn't seem to stop herself. "Did you know you dragged me out of the water? You saved my life. We collapsed on the sand together, your arms still around me. That's where they found us. They couldn't really tell who was driving."

Quinn shook her head. "I can't take all this in. I can't believe you'd let me . . ."

Laurel started to cry noisily. "Because I didn't want to think I'd done it. It was easier for me to believe it was you. I told myself it was true so often I almost began to believe it. As long as I had my damage control." She held up her drink.

Rachel took a couple of steps forward before she'd realized she'd moved. She was beyond caring if Quinn or Laurel saw her. All she could feel was Quinn's pain at Laurel's betrayal.

Quinn had sunk down on the seat again, and Laurel

walked over to her, put her arms around Quinn, pulled her against her, held Quinn's face into her breast.

"I'm sorry, Quinn. It all got out of hand. Once it started I couldn't stop it. Please say you forgive me? That you understand? There's no need to tell anyone now. It's past."

"I don't . . . I can't . . ." Quinn put Laurel away from her and stood up. She took a deep breath. "Go back inside, Laurel. I need to be by myself."

Rachel walked up the step under the pergola, and the two women turned toward her, Quinn's face pale and drawn.

"Quinn?" Rachel swallowed the lump in her throat. "Are you all right?"

Laurel flashed her bright artificial smile. "Oh, Rachel. Hi! Quinn's being a trifle antisocial, I'm afraid. She vants to be alone," she drawled the famous words and giggled at her joke.

Rachel felt a surge of unadulterated anger radiate toward the other woman. She wanted to physically lash out at her, flay her, make her pay for what she'd done to Quinn. But before she could move, Quinn was beside her, a stilling hand on her arm.

"It's okay, Rachel." Quinn's fingers wrapped around Rachel's wrist, her fingers cool on Rachel's heated skin. "Laurel was just going inside."

"But —"

Before she could finish, an imperious voice cut through the charged air between them.

"Laurel? Where the hell are you?" Mike Greenwood called exasperatedly.

Laurel drew herself together, put the bottle she held down on the seat out of sight. "I'm here, darling."

Mike bounded up onto the deck, his eyes going piercingly to his wife. "Christ, Laurel. I didn't know where the fuck you were. Have you forgotten what this evening's all about?"

"No, Mike, I haven't forgotten. I was just chatting to Quinn and Rachel. About old times."

Her husband seemed to remember he had an audience,

159

and he turned on his charming smile, infusing his voice with a more humoring tone. "Ah. That explains it. I know what you women are like when you get together." He took Laurel's arm. "But I'm afraid I'll have to kidnap my wife. I need her inside with me. She'll have to have a gossip with her girlfriends some other time. Excuse us."

He pulled Laurel along with him, and she almost tripped on the step. He steadied her and walked off with her.

"I'm sorry, darling. I didn't realize I'd been away so long." Laurel purred.

"For fuck's sake, Laurel, pull yourself together. You look like a lush," Mike exclaimed as they disappeared.

Rachel turned to Quinn, touched her cheek gently before withdrawing her hand. "Are you okay?"

"How much did you hear?"

"Enough to want to —" Rachel shook her head angrily.

"I can't feel anything. I'm completely numb." Quinn shook her head again. "I've carried this aching pain of guilt around in my chest all these years. Now I don't know what to feel."

Rachel put her arms around Quinn, held her lightly, comfortingly. They stood like that until Quinn gave a shuddering sigh. She looked up at Rachel.

"I think I want to go home," she said softly.

"We'll find Phil and Ken, get a taxi if they want to stay."

They walked silently back to the veranda, not touching, and Rachel felt as though she was operating by remote control. When they went back inside, the crowd of bodies and the roar of conversation seemed a century away, as though they'd traveled light-years to get back. Ken suddenly materialized beside them, and he gave them both a probing look. "You two okay?"

"We're both a little tired," Rachel said. "We thought we might call it a night."

"Yeah. Phil and I have had enough as well," he agreed, and Rachel felt some of her tension lessen. "I was just coming to find you. Phil's gone out to get the car. How's that for timing?"

"Wonderful." Rachel made herself smile, and she gently took Quinn's arm as they headed out the front entrance.

Phil pulled up, and he jumped out and began opening doors. Rachel helped Quinn into her seat, then she slid into the back beside her. She felt Phil give her a surprised look, but he made no comment. Without a word Ken climbed into the front beside Phil, and they headed home. Only Rachel and Phil attempted any desultory small talk on the drive to Rachel's house.

Phil stopped the car and they climbed out. As Quinn started up the path to the house Rachel paused, remembering to thank Phil for playing chauffeur.

"No worries," he said. "And Rachel. About tomorrow. I'll be there to open up. Just come in when you're ready." His gave Quinn's retreating back a fleeting, sympathetic glance. "You both look beat."

"Thanks, Phil. We'll see you both."

Quinn was waiting at the door, and once inside the house Rachel led her upstairs.

"Shower and bed, I think," she said as lightly as she could.

Quinn looked down at the buttons on her waistcoat as though she'd never seen them before.

Rachel moved her into the *en suite*, helped her undress, put her under the shower. She quickly shed her own clothes and climbed in after her. Quinn stood as Rachel soaped her body, rinsed off the suds. Then Rachel washed herself and climbed out, quickly toweling herself dry.

She went into the bedroom, and when she returned with two fresh nightshirts Quinn was still standing under the shower. Rachel turned off the water, drew Quinn out, and gently dried her. She slipped the nightshirt over Quinn's head and took her back into the bedroom. She folded down the sheets and bedspread, and when Quinn had stretched out she pulled the sheet over her and slipped in beside her.

"Quinn?" she said softly, and Quinn turned to her then.

"Just hold me, Rachel," she said brokenly. Rachel wrapped her in her arms, her lips pressed against Quinn's forehead.

They fell asleep in each other's arms, and when Rachel woke she was looking into Quinn's clear gray eyes.

"Oh." Rachel said, slightly disconcerted. "You're awake." She grimaced. "Yes, your eyes are open so you must be awake."

Quinn smiled tiredly. "Not necessarily. But in this case I am awake."

Rachel brushed a strand of dark hair from Quinn's forehead. "Feel okay?"

"Better." A frown touched Quinn's brow. "But it all seems so unreal. I still can't quite believe Laurel could have done what she did." She closed her eyes as though she was trying to blank out the memory, and Rachel kissed her gently.

Quinn sighed and opened her eyes. "Unless I dreamed it all?"

"No. It was real enough."

"How much did you hear?" Quinn asked.

"Pretty much all of it," Rachel said carefully.

Quinn sat up, wrapped her arms around her knees. "You think I should tell the police what Laurel told me?" she asked flatly.

"I don't know. I guess it's your call."

"Even if you told them what you overheard, she could certainly declare she was drunk and didn't know what she was saying."

"But surely if push came to shove Graham would tell the truth."

Quinn shrugged. "Graham's never been back here. Laurel mentioned when she came to the Garden Center that first time that someone said he was in the UK." Quinn leaned back on her elbow and looked at Rachel. "Of course, the sixty-four-thousand-dollar question is, if I did decide to tell the police everything, what would it achieve?"

"It would clear your name."

Quinn laughed softly. "It might take more than one confession to make me respectable, wouldn't you say?"

Rachel put her hand on Quinn's shoulder, rubbed it tenderly. "Those who count don't need a confession."

Quinn took Rachel's hand, rubbed it against her cheek. "Thank you. For your faith. And . . ." Quinn looked down at Rachel's hand, her fingers absently smoothing Rachel's skin. "But I guess I keep asking myself if it, if anything, would give me back those years?"

"Nothing could do that." Rachel's heart ached for Quinn.

"That's what I keep telling myself." Quinn frowned. "At the moment it seems enough that the weight of guilt I've been carrying around has been lifted from me. I just feel so much lighter. Freer."

Before Rachel could comment the phone rang, making them both jump. Rachel reached out and picked up the receiver.

"Rachel Weston."

"It's Laurel Greenwood here."

Rachel's hand tightened on the receiver. She could scarcely believe it. But it was Laurel's voice all right. What on earth . . .?

"I'm sorry to disturb you so early, Rachel, but Quinn's phone is apparently not connected yet, and I need to speak to her urgently."

Subconsciously Rachel realized that Laurel's voice gave no indication that she had been drinking heavily the night before. She sounded tired, but if Rachel hadn't seen the other woman swaying down the path with her husband she would never have suspected Laurel had been drunk.

"Nothing's wrong, is it?" Rachel asked guardedly.

"Well, no. Not exactly. Not now. It's just that the police will be calling to see Quinn sometime today, and I wanted to warn her."

"The police?" Rachel turned to look at Quinn, and Quinn straightened, motioning for Rachel to pass her the phone.

"Ah, Quinn's just come in, Laurel. I'll put her on." Rachel handed Quinn the receiver.

Rachel felt as though her whole body was held immobile, a hundred questions flitting through her mind.

"You told the police?" Quinn said into the phone, looking at Rachel in amazement.

Quinn listened, rarely spoke, until eventually she said a quiet good-bye and handed Rachel the phone to return to its cradle.

"Laurel didn't confess, did she?" Rachel asked.

"Apparently. After they got home from the reception she had a fight with Mike. He threw her into the shower to sober her up and then went to bed. She said she just got in the car and drove down to the police station. She said she couldn't live with the guilt any longer." Quinn paused. "She said she was sorry."

Rachel was speechless.

"The police called Mike, and he got a lawyer and was ranting and raving about Laurel being out of her mind and not knowing what she was saying. It must have been a circus."

They looked at each other for long moments.

"And it will continue being just that if Laurel insists on taking it further. Can you imagine, Rachel? It'll be like the last time all over again," Quinn said and rubbed her temples. "I'll have to think about it, what it all means. I don't know if I can go through it again."

"It seems Laurel's taken it out of your hands."

"Maybe I can tell them I don't want to press charges or something. I don't want Katie to have to . . . God, Rachel! What will I do?"

"Whatever you decide to do, I want you to know you don't have to do it on your own." Rachel swallowed. "I'll support you in whatever decision you make."

Quinn turned to Rachel, pushed her gently back against the pillows. "Thank you. For that. And for everything. Rachel, I don't know how to say this. I . . ."

Rachel's heart sank. A million scenarios played in her mind. Was Quinn going to tell her she'd rather go it alone? A small part of Rachel knew she couldn't condemn Quinn for that. Having to face the whole thing again was stressful enough in itself without the added burden of a fledgling romance to contend with: Who could blame Quinn if she decided it was all just too complicated?

Chapter Eighteen

"I love you."

Rachel turned back to look at Quinn. She couldn't seem to breathe. Had she heard Quinn say those three wonderful words, or was it simply wishful thinking?

"I've loved you for the longest time. I want you to know that. But I also don't want to put any pressure on you, Rachel. I know you have the kids to consider. And I have Katie. If you'd rather we kept . . ." Quinn shook her head. "I'll understand if you think we should keep our relationship . . ."

Rachel felt a surge of joy that was almost a physical pain. She wanted to crush Quinn to her, cover her with kisses, never let her go. "Our little secret?"

"Well. Yes. Or even if you want to cool it for a while."

"I thought you didn't want a furtive affair," she said thickly.

Quinn held her gaze. "I don't. I want to be honest. I want everyone to know what I feel for you, Rachel. But I also know a relationship is about two people, not just one. And I'm not sure how you see this, well, what we have between us."

"I do have concerns about us," Rachel said carefully. She felt Quinn withdraw slightly, and Rachel slid her arms around her, held her close. "Please, Quinn. Let me finish. I can't pretend not to be worried about how people will see us. My family. Yours. Our friends. But I guess the kids, the three kids, and how they'll cope with it, are my main concern. And I know it won't be easy.

"But I think we could work it out, be a loving family. All families, gay and straight, have their ups and downs, but . . ." Rachel took a steadying breath. "What I'm trying to say is, I don't want to give us up."

Quinn's face was pale. "You don't?"

"No. I don't. I've been in love with you for years," Rachel said simply. "And I don't want to lose you. Not a second time."

"A second time?"

Rachel touched Quinn's warm cheek with her finger. "Last night, Laurel said . . . Did you really have a crush on me back at school?"

Quinn gave a quick, rueful grin. "A mammoth crush. I used to dream about what I'd, well, that I'd carry you off, make mad passionate love to you." She sobered. "I wanted to be your knight, or whatever the female equivalent is, on a white charger."

"I wish you'd told me back then. I'd have climbed a tower, looked distressed." Rachel stifled a giggle, and Quinn rolled her eyes.

"Looked distressed, indeed. And as for telling you how I felt, well, I was game for any outrageous escapade. Anything except that. Just thinking about it made me weak in the knees."

"And made your stomach churn," Rachel added. "I felt the same way."

"You mean, back then?" Quinn asked incredulously. "Way back then?"

Rachel nodded. "I don't suppose you'll remember, but one day you scraped your knee after a game and you went back for another shower. The gym teacher sent me in to get you. I found you half wrapped in a towel, and I wanted to . . ."

"I do remember. Vividly. And believe me I wanted you to, too."

"But you were so cool, so self-possessed."

"You didn't see me after you left. I nearly keeled over and bloodied my other knee."

Rachel laughed. "What a pair of . . ."

Quinn let her fingertip linger on Rachel's lips. "I still had a thousand demons to lay to rest. The time wasn't right for us then, Rachel."

"It wasn't right for either of us. I certainly didn't have the courage to fly in the face of convention." Rachel sighed. "I was a colossal coward. I ran straight into the arms of Rob and the safety and the respectability of marriage."

"While I chose unrespectability." She grimaced. "Or it chose me."

"Quinn Farrelly. The wild one," Rachel said softly.

"They did call me that, didn't they?" Quinn's mouth quirked.

"But that's in the past." Rachel reminded her.

"For some people it will always hold true." Quinn looked solemnly at Rachel. "Have you considered that, Rachel? No matter what Laurel says, I'll always have my past tagging right along with me."

Rachel recalled her mother's reticence. Then she thought about her cousins, Colleen and Sandy. *Can a leopard change its spots*? Colleen had asked. But Sandy had declared no matter what Rachel was, it wouldn't make any difference to her. She weighed all this against her love for Quinn.

"That will have to be their problem," she said firmly.

"And after last night I'll be advising everyone not to mess with Rachel Weston." Quinn feigned amazement. "I thought you were going to attack Laurel."

"I'm sorry. I'm not usually like that. I've never considered myself to be a physical person, but I was so angry with Laurel."

"I could see that." Quinn raised her eyebrows at Rachel. "I thought I was supposed to be the one riding the white charger." She paused. "While I was watching you sleeping this morning, I was thinking about you racing in to champion me last night. The way you came rushing to my defense. No one's ever done that for me before. Not like that. I fell in love with you all over again."

Rachel felt the warmth of a flush wash her face. "When did you, well, first realize . . .?"

"That I was in love with you?" Quinn finished, the look in her eyes making Rachel's heartbeats tumble all over themselves, and she nodded.

"Actually it was the morning of my interview."

"That first day?" Rachel was astounded.

"Yes. I knew you owned the business, and Old Dave had told me you did the hiring. So I was prepared to see you. I just wasn't so prepared for how I'd feel when I did.

"I knew I was attracted to you straightaway, but when you were talking on the phone to Rose and you smiled" — Quinn shook her head — "I felt like I'd been hit right about here." She indicated her solar plexus, and Rachel laughed softly.

"I was just recovering from that when you took me out to look over the Garden Center. You got all enthusiastic and your face lit up, and your eyes . . . Wow! I could have happily drowned in those flashing eyes. I knew I was in trouble big time." Quinn looked at Rachel. "How about you?"

"Pretty much the same. Only I hadn't had a chance to look at your résumé, so I wasn't forewarned. And when you appeared I just . . . That was it. Try as I may to deny it, I knew my life would never be the same."

"I wish you'd given me just a slight indication you felt like that." Quinn chastised easily. "I was terrified I'd do something, say something out of place and spoil our friendship. I didn't want to do that."

Rachel nodded. "I felt the same. That night we were in the pool and it stormed. I wanted you so much."

Quinn rolled her eyes. "I reckon we were responsible for that storm, with all the electricity we were creating. I knew I couldn't stay and not touch you that night, so I left you. That was a very long night."

"The longest night of my life too."

Quinn laughed, leaned forward, kissed Rachel tenderly on the lips. She lowered herself onto Rachel, and their kiss deepened. When they drew apart they were both breathless.

Quinn glanced at the bedside clock and groaned. "We have to get ready for work soon."

Rachel leaned over and nibbled Quinn's bare shoulder where her nightshirt had slipped down. "Didn't I tell you Phil said last night that he'd open up, that we wouldn't have to rush in."

"He did? Phil is a treasure."

Rachel looked up at Quinn. "You know, I used to think you fancied him."

"You did? And I was busy worrying that he fancied you. Then I realized neither of us had the right equipment for him."

"Right equipment?" Rachel raised her eyebrows.

"Phil's gay."

"Gay?" Rachel was taken aback. "Are you sure?" Even as

she voiced the words, a hundred small incidents, half comments, fell into place. "Phil's gay," she repeated, knowing that answered a lot of her unspoken questions.

"He told me one afternoon when we were talking about relationships, about broken hearts." Quinn looked a little sheepish. "I asked him straight out if he had something going with you. Then he asked me straight out if I wanted to have something going with you. One thing led to another, and we both confessed. He's actually got it bad for Ken."

"Ken?" That did astound Rachel. She wouldn't have thought . . . "Is Ken . . .? Does Ken feel the same way?"

"I'm not sure, but I think so." Quinn shrugged faintly. "But Phil also told me he's not ready to come out to his family." She grinned mischievously. "What do you suppose everyone would say if we all came out together? Wouldn't that set the tongues awagging? They'd think there was something in the water out at the Garden Center."

"They might close us down," Rachel said, only half joking.

"Or turn the place into a shrine, and lesbians and gays from all over the world could come and pay homage." Quinn laughed out loud at Rachel's expression. "That was a joke."

"Very funny." Rachel tried to be serious and failed. She chuckled. "You know, you're very perky for someone who's in a vulnerable position here in my arms. And in my bed."

"I guess I'll just have to let you have your wicked way with me." Quinn kissed Rachel, nuzzled her ear.

Rachel felt her senses leap inside her. She took hold of Quinn's nightshirt and helped her slip it over her head, dropping it on the floor by the bed. Then she discarded her own.

Quinn gazed at her, her eyes darkening. "Well, if it's okay with Phil, I think we might take an extra half-hour," she said softly, and Rachel exclaimed indignantly.

"Half an hour?" She cupped Quinn's breast with her hand, her fingers teasing the rosy peak to attention. "Methinks my lady doth underestimate her glorious technique."

171

"I do?"

"Oh yes. You do." Rachel breathed huskily. "We'll need much, much longer than that."

"What can I say? Except, perhaps, you're the boss."

"And I say there's a little project here that I need your experienced help with, my wild, wild one." Rachel replaced her fingers with her lips, and Quinn groaned.

"I think we should talk about who drives who wild," Quinn said, and Rachel let her other hand slip down over Quinn's stomach.

"Later," she whispered thickly as her fingers found the wet warmth.

"Much, much later." Quinn agreed, her body arching, surrendering to Rachel's seductive touch.